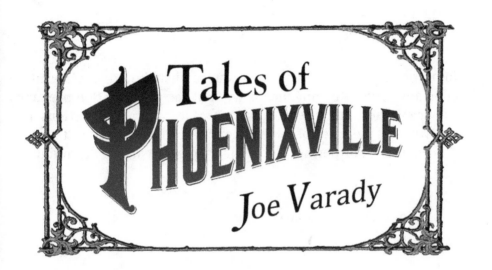

Tales of PHOENIXVILLE

Joe Varady

Cover design: Joe Varady

Editor: Carol Riley

Illustrations: Joe Varady

Chapter header font: "Back-to-Black" from mistifonts.com

Tales of Phoenixville / Joe Varady

ISBN-978-1-7369109-1-7

~ *Dedication* ~

My Great Grandfather, Andrew Varady

Váradi András was born in 1877 in the village of Dombrád, Hungary. Though his family was relatively well-to-do, András forfeited his family inheritance and defied his parents' wishes to fulfill his lifelong dream of becoming an American. In 1899, at just 22, András crossed the Atlantic aboard a ship bound for America, where he changed his name to Andrew and made his way to Phoenixville, PA. There, he lived with nine fellow countrymen in a small row home on Cinder Street, now known as Walnut Street. Andy, as he came to be called by family and friends, spent many years toiling as a day laborer at the Phoenix Iron Works. His descendants still live in and around Phoenixville.

~ Acknowledgements ~

Thank you to my father, Joseph Varady Sr. (1942-2010), who first introduced me to the importance and joy of local history, to my wife Kathy Varady for her on-going encouragement and support of all my projects, and to my son and daughter for the same. Special appreciation goes to my long-time friend, Carol Riley, for her tireless editing work on this project and aid in its publication. Thanks also to Madeline Rawley Crouse, Andrea Hilborn, Chuck and Joanne Cantwell, Robert Wood Suiter, Jack Ertell, Paul Kusko, Marjory Rohrbach, Mary Foote, Barry Taglieber, and Ed Naratil. Thank you also to John Keenan for letting me scan his amazing collection of Phoenixville postcards, one of which graces the cover of this book.

I also owe a great debt of gratitude to Phoenixville's original historian, Samuel Whitaker Pennypacker. His wonderful tome, *Annals of Phoenixville and Its Vicinity: from the Settlement to the Year 1871,* is a true treasure trove of local history and was a major inspiration for this book.

~ Table of Contents ~

~ Preface ~

To set the tone for our tales, it helps to gain some perspective by taking an imaginary trip back in time. So, humor me for a moment. Sit quietly and contemplate *where* and, perhaps more importantly, *when* you are. Imagine, if you can, what your home and its land looked like a hundred years ago. It might not have even existed then, but if your house was built a hundred years ago, agreeably life in it was very different than it is today. Now, go back even further in time and think of who cleared the land originally to build your home and what it must have been like standing in what is now your yard, your driveway, or your street when the land was in its natural state. What people first came to hunt on your land and called it *their* home?

Now, let's go back ten thousand years earlier in time. What a strange and inhospitable world your yard would have been, except it wouldn't have been *your* yard. In fact, you would most likely find that a saber-toothed tiger, wooly mammoth, or equally exotic ice age creature claimed pretty much the same spot in which you sit right now and called this spot *its* home. And, it would have been right.

Go back some 75 to 100 million years even more, and you would find your home to be the abode of even stranger creatures, this time of the dinosaur variety. Triceratops and T-Rex lived out their lives in the very place where you now dwell safely. Even farther back in time, your home would have been a swampy place full of giant ferns and three-foot dragonflies or perhaps 50 feet underwater at the bottom of a shallow inland sea.

Whether you realize it or not, the place you now call home has a deep and astonishing history. If that place happens to be a little town called Phoenixville, located in southeastern Pennsylvania, you are in for a treat. In your hands, *right now*, is a window into its past, one full of natural and national history. *So, get ready to take a trip through time...*

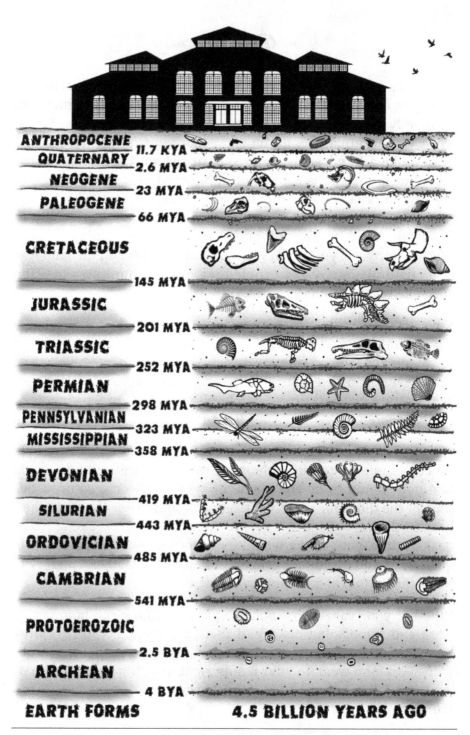

ANTHROPOCENE — 11.7 KYA
QUATERNARY — 2.6 MYA
NEOGENE — 23 MYA
PALEOGENE — 66 MYA

CRETACEOUS — 145 MYA

JURASSIC — 201 MYA

TRIASSIC — 252 MYA

PERMIAN — 298 MYA
PENNSYLVANIAN — 323 MYA
MISSISSIPPIAN — 358 MYA

DEVONIAN — 419 MYA
SILURIAN — 443 MYA
ORDOVICIAN — 485 MYA

CAMBRIAN — 541 MYA

PROTOEROZOIC — 2.5 BYA

ARCHEAN — 4 BYA

EARTH FORMS   4.5 BILLION YEARS AGO

~ Introduction ~
Our Geologic Past

Sometime in the last 15 billion years, since our universe exploded out of apparent nothingness, a star was born. It formed from the agonizingly slow coalescing of countless trillions of scattered minute particles until, finally, it self-ignited under its immense mass and shone brightly into the darkness of space. This event happened over and over again throughout the new universe as other stars were born. However, the interesting thing about this particular ball of burning gas is that you and I, and everything that we will ever know, began in the heart of this nameless star. There, within the fiery furnace of its interior, new and more complex elements were forged. That sun burned for billions of years until it eventually became unstable and exploded. The resulting supernova sent material spewing across the vacuum of space, only to have some of it coalesce, this time into a configuration with which we are far more familiar – our very own planet, Earth.

Four billion years ago, the Earth began as a fiery ball of gas and molten liquid. Slowly, it began to cool and condense, taking on solid form. Scientists know what our planet was like by studying the rocks beneath our feet and have separated our history into divisions, known as eras and periods, which are characterized by certain kinds of fossils. These eras can be thought of as the chapters of a book about the earth's history. When land is created, history is recorded in the rocks, but when land erodes that history is lost like pages that have been ripped from a book. Luckily, not all the land has eroded away, and different places record different parts of the story. Even when rock of a particular era weathers away, scientists can still make reasonable guesses at what that place would have been like using nearby geologic deposits from that same period.

In Phoenixville, the geologic book of history goes all the way back to the Permian period, about 280 million years ago, when the east coast of North America was still connected to North Africa. All continents were part of one large landmass called Pangea. Eventually, the continents broke and drifted apart. Eons passed, and the swamps became inland seas, eventually receding to become dry land once more. Dinosaurs evolved and ruled the Earth for millions of years only to meet their end some 65 million years ago. Their disappearance set the stage for the rise of mammals whose kind would, in turn, conquer the planet.

Life here went on at a slow, natural pace for millions of years. Then, sometime in the last 30,000 years or so, a new species arrived, mankind. And this is when our tales of Phoenixville begin.

Some of Phoenixville's Former Inhabitants:

Left to Right: Meganeura (giant dragonfly), Carboniferous Period, 350 million years ago; **Edaphosaurus (sail back),** Early Permian Period, 270 million years ago; **Dryptosaurus (tyrannosauroid),** Late Cretaceous Period, 70 million years ago; **Woolly Mammoth,** Pleistocene Period, 2 million years ago; **Smilodon (saber-toothed cat),** Pleistocene Period, 2 million years ago; **Homo Sapiens,** Late Pleistocene Period, around 16,000 years ago.

~ Chapter One ~

New Arrivals:
The Tale of the Ice Age Hunters

16,000 BC: North America is in the midst of the Pleistocene Ice Age. To the north, huge barren ice sheets, nearly a mile thick, cover the landscape. Just south of these ice sheets, the green hills are home to a variety of large animals.

Joral moved slowly and quietly through the trees, his eyes occasionally moving from side to side to be sure he kept pace and position with the other hunters. Their prey was not far ahead and not difficult to track. The enormous beast trampled the undergrowth flat wherever he went and left a heavy trail of blood from the spears stuck in him.

Joral and his tribe were Paleo-Indians, members of a pre-Clovis culture that included the first humans to inhabit North America during the Pleistocene epoch, a time when mile-high glaciers covered much of North America. His people were hunter-gatherers who lived a nomadic life. Their usual quarry consisted of small game such as turtles, rabbits, and deer, but occasionally they hunted larger prey such as bison and even the largest of animals, the wooly mammoth. Although the men of Joral's tribe had taken at least one mammoth a year for as long as they could remember, never before had they ever taken down a mammoth as large and impressive as the one that they were pursuing now. Joral was certain that stories about this hunt would be told around the fire for many years to come and that his name would be part of the telling. The idea of being included in the songs would have thrilled him as a younger man, but Joral was older now, and wiser. He was no longer an unproven hunter whose position in the tribe was not yet secure, one who was always trying to impress his father, the older hunters, the other boys, and of course, the girls - or at least the girls who were yet to be spoken for. For Joral, it was enough these days just to survive a hunt, to wake to another sunrise, and to hold his woman and child as they sat around the fire each night.

The small group of six hunters set out three days ago from their base camp, many miles to the west, following a winding creek. The creek bore no name, as no member of their tribe had ever laid eyes upon it before. People who would live here later would name it "Sankanac," and, later still, others would call it "French Creek." These hunters, however, had no interest in naming it; they were simply passing through. Nor were they interested in the several opportunities of bison and elk that they quietly passed by. They all knew what they were after on *this* hunt. Another summer passed, brown leaves were already beginning to fall gently from the trees, and though it had not been spoken, they knew that they were looking for a wooly mammoth and, more importantly, that nothing else would do. Joral was as excited as everyone else, but his excitement was tempered. He was old enough to have learned a lesson his father taught him, "Be careful what you wish for, Joral, as you may find it."

Earlier that morning, the hunters awakened with the sun as they did each day and ate a quick breakfast of dried meat and berries, washing it down with cold water from the creek. In the early morning mist, they quietly rolled their sleeping furs into tight bundles, tying them snugly with leather thongs before slinging them over their shoulders. Once assembled, the men nodded to each other and set off in single file, a few paces apart, spears ready in hand. It wasn't long before they saw the tracks again, large, round, and unmistakable, in the sand along the creek's edge. The hunters did not speak, but they all saw and knew it would not be long before they found what they were seeking.

The line of men kept the stream on their left, sometimes losing sight of it for a while only to find it again as it wound its way along a stony bed at the bottom of a shallow vale, tucked in among the gently rolling hills of what would someday be called Pennsylvania. Three days journey to the north, a great wall of ice towered over the land. It was so unbelievably high that the top was often lost in the clouds. Beyond the wall was a frozen wasteland where snow fell but never melted. Below the tower of ice, a wide savannah extended south until, eventually, trees and forests grew. It was along this boundary of forest and prairie that Joral's tribe lived off the land. Traveling just south of the ice sheets, they gathered plants, hunted, and fished. They were hearty people who did not require much to be happy. During the summer months, the band of 40 or so men, women, and children moved from place to place frequently. However, when fall arrived, they sought protected locations, such as rock overhangs, where they could build sturdy shelters to wait out the cold, dark months of winter, laughing with friends and family around a warm fire.

Another summer was coming to an end, and it was time for one last big hunt before winter preparations could begin in earnest. Joral traveled light on the hunt. On one hip hung his bundled sleeping skins, on the other a hide bag. In the bag were a flint knife, some dried bison meat, and a high-energy mixture of fat and berries that he stored in a hollow gourd container. The hunters did not carry water, which was one reason they stayed close to the stream. Another reason was that animals searching for water often wore paths along the creeks making traveling by foot easier.

Like many animals, the mammoths visited rivers and streams regularly to drink, and these hunters learned it was best to attack them in swampy areas. Caught in the mud, the beast's great weight would work against it, slowing it down and allowing the hunters to get close enough to kill it quickly. There was little room for error when hunting mammoths. Towering more than twice the height of a man and weighing thousands of pounds, the much smaller hunters needed every advantage that they could get against their enormously powerful prey, which could crush them in an instant.

The risk was worth it, though. If successful, every one of the hunters knew that their dangerous labors would be rewarded with enough meat to ensure their entire tribe plenty of food, enough to sustain them through even the harshest winter.

In Joral's bag were four sharp spear tips, each wrapped in its own leather wallet to protect the razor-sharp stone head. The spearheads were chipped, or knapped, skillfully to a point with a flute, or groove, running down its length. Many millennia later, very different men would call these spearheads "Clovis points." A stick split at the end was slid over the grooves on either side of the point, lashed on tightly with animal sinew, and sealed with pine resin. The tips fit neatly into the ends of longer spear shafts of which each hunter carried two.

In order to throw his spears with enough power to kill a mammoth and from far enough away to live to tell the tale, Joral used an atlatl, an arm's length piece of wood with a cup carved onto one end. The butt of the spear was placed into the cup, essentially lengthening the arm of the hunter and giving the thrown spear increased speed and power. The fluted spear point was thin and razor-sharp. It could easily penetrate the thick hide of a mammoth. Ideally, the point would lodge deep inside the giant beast's body, while the shaft would fall away to be recovered and used again.

When the hunters finally came across the herd of mammoths they were tracking, they found them grazing in an open field across the stream. There were at least seven of them in the herd, sharing the clearing with two slow-moving giant ground sloths. The sloths were spending the day as always, standing on their hind legs, grasping branches leisurely with the long, curved claws on their front paws and using their long, black tongues to snake out and strip the leaves from the branch. With the help of thick lips, they pulled them into their wide mouths to be ground into pulp by large flat molars powered by massive jaw muscles. The hunters never bothered hunting sloths. Relatives of armadillos, they had a bony hide that could turn a spear. Mammoths were far better prey.

Mammoths usually traveled in small family units. A typical mammoth family consisted of an older matriarch, three or four adult daughters, and several calves. These females lived together to help each other with the birth and care of their young. Together, they ensured the protection of their calves by keeping them surrounded at all times. Male calves grew up in these family units, but upon reaching maturity, left their old herd to join all-male bachelor pods. When a bull desired to mate, he left his bachelor pod, sought out a herd of elephant cows, and mated with a willing female. Afterwards, he returned to the other males, having nothing to do with the rearing or caring of his young.

The hunters would have preferred a herd of females, but instead, they stumbled upon a herd of big bulls. The smallest was an impressive ten feet tall, and the largest towered at least another two feet more. Each animal possessed a pair of massive tusks and a trunk as big around as a man's torso. Once more, his father's words echoed in his ears, "Be careful what you wish for, Joral."

The hunters spent the better half of the day carefully observing the herd, coming up with a workable plan, and maneuvering into position. The land in the immediate area was dry and the creek bed was stony. There was no spot swampy enough to bog a mammoth down, so they would have to improvise. They found a place along the path at a bend in the creek where the water undercut the bank, resulting in a drop of several feet into the water. Joral and three other hunters went downstream, crossed the creek, and worked their way stealthily back up the mammoth trail stamped out on the other side. Once at the overhang, they set an ambush to surprise one of the beasts, planning to drive it over the ledge and into the water. As the animal stumbled in the creek, the hunters would close on it from both banks, driving their spears into it and killing it before it could regain a sure footing and put up a fight or flee. To Joral and the other hunters, it sounded like a good plan.

Joral and two of the other hunters hid in the brush on a slope leading down to the creek. There, they waited for their prey to come through. Another hunter hid farther down the path, closer to the trail. Female mammoth herds moved together as a group in an orderly single file, but bull herds were much less predictable. It took nearly three hours, but their patience was finally rewarded. Joral felt the great beast coming before he heard it, and he heard it long before he saw it. Joral could tell that it was big, and as fate would have it, along came what surely must have been the oldest and largest bull in the herd. The huge mammoth towered well over twelve feet tall and carried a pair of large, scarred tusks that seemed out of proportion, even on this behemoth. Joral wondered if it would be wiser to just let this one pass. Unfortunately, he had no time to communicate these thoughts to his brothers; their plan was already in motion. He would just have to play his part and hope that they got lucky.

Just as the giant lumbered into position between Joral and the creek, the hunter waiting down the path jumped out and began yelling. He waved a long pine bough over his head in an attempt to make himself look larger and more intimidating than he was, and the plan worked. The surprised bull stopped dead in its tracks, clearly taken aback by the strange obstruction in its way. The startled beast tried to turn itself around on the narrow path, but as it did, Joral and the other hunters leapt up, letting their spears fly.

They chose their ambush site well and were in a good position. All three spears flew true and struck deep into the giant's hairy flank, causing it to recoil in pain and surprise. Its enormous rear foot stumbled, the soft soil of the overhang crumbled, and the huge beast bellowed as it began to fall backwards, seemingly in slow motion, over the edge of the embankment. The monster landed on its back in the creek with a thunderous splash that sent water flying in all directions.

The hunters on the far bank sprang suddenly from their hiding places and let fly two more spears at the now terrified mammoth. These should have been simple shots, yet, somehow, neither spear found its mark. The old mammoth rolled to its feet and began throwing water in all directions.

Experience showed now in Joral's smooth, automated reactions. He had his second spear cradled already in his atlatl and was charging down the hill, his arm chambering high behind his head before his companions scarcely moved. As he reached the bank, Joral saw that he had a perfect shot, and he took it. He barely slowed down, adding the momentum of his run to the speed and power of his spear, which sank deep into the creature's backside.

His strike came just in time to keep the hairy beast from charging his companions, who now found themselves exposed on the opposite bank. The huge mammoth wheeled, turned its great head to one side, and looked straight at Joral with huge, brown eyes that seethed with fiery anger. Joral was shocked to also see intelligence in its eyes, something he recognized as almost *human*. His thoughts were suddenly interrupted as the giant trumpeted deafeningly, kicked off, and thundered away downstream, leaving the hunters looking at each other dumbfounded for a moment, before collecting their spears and running off in pursuit of their prey.

The old bull took flight down the streambed and was quickly lost to sight around a bend. Where shallow enough, the smaller humans could run in the water, but where the creek was deeper, they took to the shore and had to find their way along its banks, slowing the hunters down. Their prey was far ahead of them now, so the hunters moved as quickly as possible along a shallow stretch of the stream, more intent on making good speed than being cautious. As they came around a bend in the creek, it was the humans' turn to stop dead in their tracks. A mixture of fear and awe washed over them. Ahead of them, lying right in the middle of the shallow creek, was the mammoth.

The colossus was facing them, resting peacefully in the creek with its eyes closed. It did not move, and its head hung limply. Only its great tusks, resting on the bottom of the shallow streambed, kept its head upright and out of the water. The hunters spread out across the creek, advancing slowly, their spears held high at the ready. With less than twenty paces to go, they paused looking for any sign of life, but the hairy giant did not stir. A generous amount of blood soaked and matted the thick hair on the creature's broad side. The hunters glanced at each other and shrugged. Thoughts of victory began to grow inside them. The hunters were just beginning to relax and lower their spears when the great brown mountain of hair lying in the stream suddenly came to life. The beast opened its eyes as it lifted its enormous head, its ivory tusks dripping clear, cold water along their incredible length. Joral had the sickly realization that they had fallen into a clever trap. The mammoth had been waiting for them.

The old giant's timing couldn't have been better. He was on his feet and charging forward almost before the startled hunters could react. The men scrambled madly to either side, but the two hunters nearest the middle of the stream were caught before they could get out of the way. The first, a strapping young man named Brun, was knocked down against the rock riverbed and trampled by the feet of the huge animal, turning the water around them a vibrant red. Then, with a sudden twist of its massive head, the mammoth caught the second hunter, Aron, square in the small of his back as he attempted to flee. The thick tusk sent him flying headfirst into the rocky bank where his limp, broken body crumbled into a heap.

The mammoth spun to find that the other four hunters were scrambling up the banks on either side of the creek. For a second, the mammoth could not decide which pair to pursue. It then turned away from Joral and his partner and thundered up the bank after the two hunters on the opposite shore. Instantly, Joral stopped running, gripping his last spear in his hand, turned, and hurled it across the creek in a futile effort to distract the beast.

Without the time to load it into his atlatl, the spear fell well short of its intended target. The mammoth stampeded away after the other two hunters as Joral rushed forward to recover his weapon. When he did, Joral glanced at his fallen brothers in the creek, men he knew since they were boys, and realized sadly that they would hunt no more.

Just then, his companion Dran rushed up and together they crossed the creek. They did not have to travel far before they could hear angry trumpeting and feel the ground shaking beneath their feet. A few steps more, a horrible scene opened up before them. Once the hunters, their other companions were now the hunted and were attempting to keep a large tree between themselves and the angry pachyderm. Each time the angry, bloody animal circled to one side, the hunters scrambled the other way. Surrounding trees hindered the great beast's movements, and it snorted loudly with frustration as it struggled to get at the men. Joral looked to Dran and, with a silent nod of agreement, they advanced.

The mammoth's attention was absorbed completely by the two hunters that were trapped behind the tree, so it did not see Joral and his partner until it was too late. They launched their spears simultaneously, striking them deep and true into the mountain of flesh. The monster wheeled about to face them, eyes blazing with fierce anger. Never before had Joral seen a mammoth behave in such a manner, and it suddenly occurred to him that this creature was acting more like a predator, like a savage saber tooth or a hungry cave bear. Reacting instinctively, he ran.

Joral pumped his legs as fast as he could, for he could hear the great angry beast charging after him through the brush. Somehow, just before he was about to be trampled underfoot, like his unfortunate brother in the stream, Joral hurtled himself to the side and barely avoided being flattened by the mammoth's huge feet as they thundered past. The behemoth did not look back or even slow down, and to Joral's great relief, thundered out of sight into the dense underbrush.

The four remaining hunters quickly regrouped. This time, they moved slowly and quietly through the trees. Joral's eyes moved from side to side, ensuring he kept pace and position with the others. Their quarry was not far ahead and not difficult to track. The spear tips, lodged deep inside his body, had surely taken their toll as evidenced by the heavy trail of blood. When the surviving hunters finally came across the great mammoth, they found it lying at the foot of a steep hill.

The creature lay on its side, its broad flank heaving with labored breath. Taking no chances this time, they stayed at a distance and hurtled their remaining spears into the dying animal. Only after they were confident it was dead did they approach their fallen adversary. Even then, it was with great caution and deep respect.

Although the mammoth was dead, Joral knew that their struggles were far from over. The mammoth was too heavy to move, let alone carry, and before daybreak, saber-toothed cats and dire wolves from miles around would come calling, each interested in claiming a share of the carcass. The night to come would prove to be as perilous as the hunt. However, with the help of fire, Joral was confident that they would persevere in defending their kill. One of the younger men was chosen to return upstream to find their tribe and lead them back here. It would be a good place for them to shelter for the winter. The tribe's camp would be moved to the location of the kill, and Phoenixville would have her very first human inhabitants.

Epilogue

The Port Kennedy Bone Cave, located in Valley Forge National Park, preserved the skeletal remains of literally thousands of ice age animals, everything from turtles, skunks, and snakes to giant ground sloths, dire wolves, saber-toothed tigers, cave bears, and of course, wooly mammoths. For over a million years, these creatures lived on the very same land that Phoenixville occupies today.

The Port Kennedy Bone Cave.

Radiocarbon dating of artifacts found at the Meadowcroft Rock Shelter in southwestern Pennsylvania, 320 miles west of Phoenixville, indicate that prehistoric hunters and gatherers, likely originating from Europe, lived there some 16,000 to 19,000 years ago. This is the oldest known site of human habitation in Pennsylvania to date. It is likely that these hunter-gatherers could have been the first humans to inhabit Phoenixville, as well. While Joral's battle with the mammoth is fictional, the hunting of large Pleistocene megafauna with stone-tipped spears did take place and must have been dangerous and unpredictable. The story of Joral is set along the French Creek, ending at the base of the steep hill leading up to the north side of Phoenixville.

~ Chapter Two ~
The First European:
The Tale of Charles Pickering

1694: Europeans are colonizing the New World, offering immense opportunities and rewards for those who are daring and adventurous enough to claim them.

Charles Pickering turned up his collar against the cold night air. He stood deep in thought at the rail of a privately commissioned ship bound for England... bound at last for home. Charles had spent the last decade or so in search of fortune and adventure in the New World. Adventure he found, but fortune had thus far eluded him. A chill spray of water caught him in the face seemingly out of nowhere as the bow of the ship cut into the crest of a large wave. He had noticed the sea getting rougher ever since he came above deck. The moon still shone brightly among a thousand twinkling stars that illuminated the edges of the low scattered clouds floating against the black velvet of the sky. Somewhat melancholy, Charles found the sight beautiful to behold and resisted the urge to retreat to his warm and dry bunk in the hold below.

As Charles Pickering continued to gaze at the sky, he thought back to his first crossing, a little over ten years before. That trip, in the summer of 1682, had been much different than this one. Aboard the *Welcome*, his first crossing had passed quickly, due in no small part to the company of his young wife, Mary. Together they shared the excitement and anticipation of unknown opportunity, a stirring excitement felt alike by many of the other passengers bound for the New World, including his friend, William Penn, who had recently received an exceptionally generous grant of land from the Crown in repayment of debts owed to his father.

Penn spent the better part of the trip sharing his many grand ideas for a new civilization, which he deemed a "Holy Experiment." Charles found his friend's discourse quite fascinating. If he heard it once, he heard it a hundred times that trip, "Charles, my friend, I may has't acted hastily when I hath sold thee 1,000 acres for only twenty pounds sterling fore even leaving England." To which Charles would politely remind him that he was part-owner of the small fleet of ships that were actively engaged in stewarding members of the Society of Friends to the New World. This included the *Welcome* upon which they sailed.

Pickering found Penn intriguing. The son of Admiral Sir William Penn of His Majesty's Royal Navy, young William attended Oxford University and was groomed as an elite aristocrat. However, he turned his back on his privileged life and chose, instead, to become a man of conscience, much to his father's chagrin. Penn was arrested for attending Quaker meetings and for becoming a staunch critic of both religion and the crown. Over and over again, William campaigned in favor of religious tolerance, protesting the unlawful confiscation of Quaker property and speaking out against the unjust imprisonment of Quakers. Charles admired Penn's audacity, and the two soon became fast friends.

"Thee, more than anyone else, knoweth what a difficult time this is for Quakers in England, Charles. Our refusal to bow or taketh thine hats off to the Crown hath accomplished little other than receiveth us into exile. While nonconformists, we remain relatively strict Christians. Therefore, I doth not believeth this alone wast not enough to earn us ye title of 'Enemies of ye Throne.' More likely 'tis our antithetical beliefs towards an absolute monarchy that touts itself to have been divinely appointed by God."

"Yea, William, refusal to taketh oaths of loyalty to ye king or payeth tithes to support ye Church of England hath made for us enemies in both camps. Once branded heretics, we becameth ye 'whipping boys' of London, blamed for every blight and plague. Thee wast lucky to have hadst thy father, ye Admiral, useth his influence from a lifetime of service to ye Crown to protect thee. Even now, that gent watches over thee from beyond ye grave. God rest his soul." With that, Charles drank down the sour contents of his wooden cup.

"We were facing a losing battle, but God provided me with a purpose. I kneweth ye Crown still owed mine father a debt of 16,000 pounds sterling, and so now to me, but I wast careful not to mention it when I tooketh ye opportunity to appeal directly to King Charles and proposed a mass emigration of Quakers to ye New World. I nev'r would have imagined his 'majesty' would deed such a vast tract of land. Previously western New Jersey, it is bordered by New York to ye north and Lord Baltimore's Maryland to ye south!"

"Instantly making thee into America's largest private landowner. Since ye land, William, is described as unbroken wilderness, I thought thy original name, 'Sylvania', was fitting. However, I admit that King Charles' amendment to 'Pennsylvania,' in honor of thy father, is more pleasing to ye ear."

"Of course, I knoweth that King Charles' motives for such a large land grant wast two-fold. If't be true, we flourish and help pave ye way for future colonization of ye New World, and if't be untrue, we perish and will no longer stir up trouble in England. After all, Quakers are quite expendable, and as thee more than anyone else knoweth, Charles, of paramount importance to England is ye acquisition of riches."

"One can hardly find blame there. Ye Spanish hast discovered gold in Central and South America. Surely, thither is gold to be found in ye north, as well. England hath yet to findeth it! Ye Jamestown colony, those gents sent to Virginia, nearly starved their first winter after spending their whole year prospecting and mining fool's gold instead of planting food. In ye end, no precious metals hadst been found, so now ye king is eager to ope' up new lands in ye north. Since he doesn't care whom he uses to make it happen, he killeth two birds with one stone, starting a much-needed colony whist at ye same time ridding himself of ye dissident Penn and his Quaker rabble. Genius, William, genius!"

"Charles, may thy experience in prospecting for precious metals help thee findeth fortune in ye wild lands of America. Ye rewards for anyone who findeth gold would be most wonderous yet alone if one hath to happen upon El Dorado."

"I place no stock in the Spaniard's legends of a City of Gold, William. I would be satisfied with a modest vein. Though I must admit, with so much unexplored land ahead and ye Spanish successes so well known, 'tis difficult not to alloweth ye imagination flare and desires soar."

"Perhaps 'tis there for thee to find, Charles. God hath most wondrous plans for Pennsylvania. I can feeleth it in mine bones! He hath blessed it and wilt maketh it ye seed of a new nation. Thither, we wilt createth a political utopia guaranteeing freedom of religion, free elections, freedom from unjust imprisonment, and free and fair trial by jury. At ye heart of this great new land, I envision a marvelous city, whither all men wilt exist as equals. I wilt calleth it, Philadelphia, ye city of brotherly love!"

"What of ye Indians, William? Wilt thee civilize them?"

Penn responded emphatically, "We must ensure that ye cruelties enacted upon ye natives by the greedy and savage Spanish conquistadors wilst not be repeated on this venture. We doth not cometh as soldiers or conquerors. Ye natives wilt be treated with ye kindness and respect due all men."

"That is valorous, William. If't be true and all goeth well, I hope to locate a valuable deposit and commence mining operations as soon as possible. Friendly relations with ye natives worketh nicely into mine plans. Ye last thing I needeth is a host of hostile savages getting between mine fortune and me!" Charles smiled as he recalled how they had both laughed heartily and drained their cups.

On October 23rd, 1682, the *Welcome* came in sight of land and a great cheer went up among all aboard. The ship sailed along the Delaware peninsula, which remained under the control of the Duke of York, until they entered a large bay that soon narrowed to a river. Finally, after nearly two months at sea, the *Welcome* made land at the port of New Castle. Some passengers, mostly small groups of immigrant families, disembarked and went their separate ways while the majority of Penn's company prepared for the next stage of their journey. Within a few days, supplies, equipment and livestock were purchased and the party was prepared to set out north along the Delaware River.

By November, they arrived at Penn's site for Philadelphia. The *Welcome* pulled into an indentation of the Delaware where a little tributary, called Dock Creek, created a convenient little cove and safe harbor for the small ship. Penn chose the site, in part, because he envisioned it would someday become a capacious and permanent dock. The Lenni-Lenape Indians, who dwelt in the nearby villages of Shakamaxon and Coaquanock, called the little inlet "Coocanonoon" and used the cove for generations before the arrival of the whites.

The *Welcome* moored at a landing along the grassy banks of the clear running creek, near a newly constructed row of houses. The building nearest the landing, on the corner of Dock and Front Street, had a tavern sign hanging out front with a bright blue anchor painted on it. Charles Pickering wondered at the progress. "William, it would seemeth the building of Philadelphia hast already begun, in earnest. I am amazed that the Quaker groups that preceedth us could have accomplished so much in only a few short months!"

Penn's first expedition had sent back detailed reports and surveys for his review. "Six Swedish families wast already living hither when our ships first arrived. They even hadst a small church. After some simple negotiations, the Swedes concurred to selleth their holdings. On mine orders, streets wast surveyed, laid out, and the construction of many new buildings beganeth."

Later that day, Charles Pickering purchased Lot 22, located on Delaware Front Street, midway from High Street (known now as Market Street) to Chestnut Street. On the property was a small house into which Charles and Mary moved and began the process of turning it into a home. Within a few weeks, they had the beginnings of a well-stocked pantry and larder, complete with a barrel of corn flour, and several cords of firewood split and stacked outside, ready to help them through the upcoming winter.

The little community seemed to have all it needed to prosper and grow, yet Penn longed to attend to one last important detail. One night in November, while sharing a dinner of turkey pie around the fire, William told Charles, "I hast no illusions that the King's land grant meaneth precious little to the native people who already calleth this land home. Therefore, I hath asked several companions to travel with me the short distance to the Lenape Indian village, Shakamaxon, wither we wilt meeteth with Chief Tammany and other tribal leaders to maketh a treaty of friendship with the Lenape people. We will purchase this land to ensureth friendly relations and peace for our colony."

A few days later, Charles accompanied Penn to the Indian village. There, under a large ancient elm tree, a solemn ceremony took place. Penn's men presented the silver coins in two ornately decorated walnut chests, and while the chests were accepted graciously, Chief Tammany and the other tribal leaders seemed far more interested in the cloth and metal trade goods that had been included. Their reaction came as no surprise to Charles, who wondered what need the natives might have for European coinage. Chief Tammany then presented Penn with a beautiful wampum belt. It consisted of thousands of small beads strung together in bold patterns of white, purple, and black. Made from the shells of a clam called the quahog, the wampum was something obviously deemed of great value by the Lenape. To Charles, this was clearly an exchange of gifts commemorating an agreement of peace between their people.

With the treaty signed and his wife, Mary, safe and snug in their new home, Charles Pickering felt he could, at last, get to his real task at hand. Prospecting meant wandering alone far into the wilds of the interior, well beyond the relative safety of their budding little hamlet. If he set out now, he should be able to return before the frigid months of January and February.

Mary readied him a large sack of dried meat and biscuits of the same kind that he endured during the long voyage across the Atlantic. In addition, he carried a leather pack containing a tinderbox, complete with flint and steel for making fires, extra clothes, a wool blanket, a hand ax, and an oilcloth to keep off the rain. Hanging on the outside of the pack was a small shovel and, of course, his prospecting pan. Charles decided to travel up a nearby river that the Dutch sailed right past several times as they explored the Delaware nearly a century before. Around 1620, someone finally noticed its mouth, hidden by a dense growth of cattails, and they named it the *Schuylkill* or "hidden river." That had been around 1620, and to Charles's knowledge no European had as yet ventured up the river very far. The Schuylkill River seemed as good a place as any to start, so, armed with only the short knife on his belt, he bid his wife and companions farewell and set off on foot in its direction.

As he traveled, Pickering frequently stopped to inspect promising outcrops of rock or pan along the water's edge. Prospecting is a matter of patient, careful, systematic searching. Therefore, whenever he came to a sandy beach where he could approach the river, he'd shuck off his pack and scoop up a pan full of material. Squatting at the river's edge, he'd carefully swirl his pan in the water, allowing heavier material to settle in the bottom of the pan and lighter material to gradually wash away in the gentle current. He hoped to find placer gold, gold found on the surface that could range anywhere from fine dust to hefty nuggets. However, he kept his eyes peeled for telltale signs of other precious metals, as well.

Pickering frequently encountered the area's resident Indians who always seemed very curious about him. At first, the natives would just point at him and whisper to each other in hushed tones whenever they spotted him squatting alongside the river as they paddled by in their long dugout canoes. He ran into them along the bank, as well, but he soon found that he had little to fear. The natives seemed friendly, and eventually, through gestures and signs, they invited him to visit them at their lodges. Curious about everything, they were especially so when it came to his metal tools. They never seemed to tire of looking at his ax, his knife, or his prospecting pan. He found the native's company pleasant, their shelters warm and comfortable, and their food much more to his liking than his meager provisions of dried meat and stale biscuits.

Over the next several weeks, Pickering made his way nearly twenty miles upriver but had little to show for his efforts. After swirling countless pans of gravel, he finally found what he was looking for when he caught a glint of something shiny in the bottom of his prospecting pan. He thought it was just a reflection of the sun in the water, at first. However, his heart skipped a beat when he saw it again. The small piece of silvery, metallic-looking crystal that his fingers pinched carefully out of his pan was not much larger than an apple seed, but it was enough. Pickering recognized it as a piece of galena, an important lead ore mineral. Galena itself was not all that valuable, but Charles knew that galena deposits often contained significant amounts of silver, as well. It was this knowledge that caused his heart to race and his hands to shake.

Charles panned that stretch of the Schuylkill River for several days until he traced its source up a smaller tributary. There, he located what looked to be a promising deposit of galena ore along the south bank of the creek. He carefully marked the spot so that he could easily find it again, before traveling back downstream to the

Schuylkill. Charles found his return much quicker, now that he did not have to pick his way along the riverbanks and stop to pan at every opportunity. He traveled along an Indian trail that followed the Gans-howe-hanne, the noisy and rushing stream, the natives' name for what the English were calling the Schuylkill River. In just a few days, he found himself emerging from the woods outside of Penn's newly founded Philadelphia.

In his absence, the number of buildings seemed to have doubled along the newly laid out grid of streets. Charles did not tarry for conversation to catch up on recent events, though, and answered with a brief, but hearty "Good day!" to those who greeted him as he came into town. He made straight for his small house by Dock Creek, where Mary greeted him with tears of joy and relief. After a long embrace, Mary fed and cleansed him so that he could seek out William to share his good news. When they met later that day, at the Governor's house, Pickering could barely contain himself and, in front of a roaring fire, he told Penn of his findings. Penn was so excited at the prospect of a province rich in silver that he granted Charles several thousand acres bordering the stream that would soon become known as Pickering's Creek.

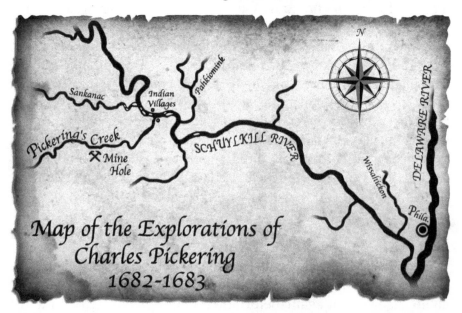

Map of the Explorations of
Charles Pickering
1682-1683

With the winter months upon them, Charles was happy to be spending some time indoors with Mary before he returned to sleeping under the stars. He needed time to plan for the next expedition and decided not to set out again until March. Charles knew that he could not take on the challenge of mining the galena ore alone, so he confided his secret to a man named Tinker that Charles knew to have experience in such matters. He also hired an ex-Benedictine monk named John Gray to conduct a survey of the ore lands along what Penn now called the Pickering Tract. After acquiring such equipment as picks and shovels, as well as provisions such as smoked ham and potatoes, the small party set off into the wilderness with two mules to help them carry the load.

When they arrived at the galena deposit Charles had located earlier, they unloaded their gear and set up camp. John Gray, who was also called Jathan, set about surveying and mapping the surrounding hills and valleys, while Pickering and Tinker set about digging. Within a few days they dug a short tunnel into the side of the hill. They arched over the roof and lined the floor with large, flat stones. Though it produced little or nothing in the way of galena ore, the cave did provide an effective shelter against the rain and the cold. Their set up complete, the two men began searching in earnest for a rich deposit of galena.

Pickering's first impressions were correct, and they soon found a vein of galena close to the surface. They mined the ore by hand, loading it into empty flour barrels. Next, they needed to figure out how to get the ore to Philadelphia, where it would be loaded onto a ship and sent to England for refining. Tinker suggested packing it on the mules, but this solution would greatly limit how much ore they could retrieve. Charles had a better idea. While preparing for the trip, he made sure to purchase extra knives and axe heads for barter and trade. Pickering now paid a visit to an Indian village located nearby on the shores of the Schuylkill River by the mouth of his creek.

Although he could not speak their language, Charles' was confident from his previous interactions with the natives that, by using a combination of gestures to communicate and using the metal tools and pack animals to barter, he would be able to make a deal with the owners of the dugout canoes he often watched trolling sleekly up and down the river. If all went as planned, he would have Tinker and himself, along with all their ore and equipment, ferried down the river all the way to Philadelphia, while Gray would stay behind and complete his survey. It happened that Pickering's hopes were well founded. There were two such canoes in the village, and the tribe's braves were more than willing to accept the exotic gifts in return for an adventurous trip with the strangers.

They filled all eight flour barrels with the best ore they could find and hauled them to the shore. In the spring of 1683, a small band of Indians helped them load the barrels and equipment into the two dugout canoes. The Lenape braves were curious as to why these strange men had come all this way just to take stones from the Earth. Nevertheless, they helped push the two canoes off into the river, each loaded with four barrels of ore, one Englishmen, and two Lenape.

Despite the fact that they sat low in the water, weighed down by the barrels and three men each, the canoes were still highly maneuverable in the skilled hands of the Indians who, with strong shoulders and wide paddles, moved deftly to avoid obstacles such as sandbars, rapids, or submerged logs, never seeming to tire. The travelers stopped on the shore only briefly to eat and to relieve themselves. Coupled with the fact that they moved downstream with the current, the strange company made amazing time and arrived at Philadelphia before the setting of the sun.

The fledgling village had only the most rudimentary necessities. The blacksmith was newly arrived and only recently set up shop with a large bellows and an anvil. He lacked the knowledge and equipment to refine the galena ore. Therefore, Charles waited several weeks for the next ship of new arrivals and much-needed supplies to come up the Delaware River. When it moored at the half-constructed docks, he arranged with its captain to have the ore shipped back to England, there to be smelted and the silver extracted from the rock. Whatever precious metal obtained in the process would then be sent back to Philadelphia, along with a report on the quality of the ore that would help Charles determine the viability of a larger venture in the hills along the Pickering Creek.

Charles figured the ocean voyage to England would take an average of two months, then another month for the ore to be processed and a return ship secured, and another two months to return to Philadelphia. He knew he could not expect any results for at least six months, but that was fine with him. Exploring the woodlands of the New World in search of fortune and treasure was exciting, but it was also exhausting work. He and Tinker worked most assiduously, and he was quite ready for a respite. Although Philadelphia left much to be desired in the way of conveniences, nights at home with his wife were decidedly better than sleeping in a cave in the wilderness with Tinker and Gray.

Pickering enjoyed watching a civilization grow out of the wilderness. William Penn's enthusiasm was quite contagious, and Charles found himself sharing Penn's interest in the law. Few cases in the early courts required much knowledge of the law or skill to hear and decide cases, or the ability to prosecute or defend those on trial. Without any special training as lawyers, men of a good education and keen wit, like Pickering, were quite equal to the tasks required and, soon Charles was admitted to the bar and began practicing in the courts.

In August of 1683, Charles was busy erecting a fence around the local Quaker graveyard when a young messenger boy found him. "Sire, a ship hath docketh carrying cargo addressed to thee. Ye captain sayeth thee would hast to claim ye package in person." Pickering's heart leapt up into his throat as he realized what it must be. He set down his shovel and excitedly followed the boy back down to the dock.

The barrel handed to him by the first mate was disappointingly small, but as he took it, Charles was surprised to find that it was heavier than it looked. He fought the urge to break it open right then and there, and instead, thanked the man and set off in search of Tinker. He found him overseeing the construction of a well. It didn't take long to convince Tinker to take a short break from his toils. They rushed to his cabin where they used a hammer and chisel to pry open the top of the barrel. With much anticipation, the two men dumped the content of the barrel on the thick boards of the table. Pickering and Tinker, eyes wide, stared down on the rewards of all their hard work out in the wilderness as several small bars of bright silver peered back at them through the saw-dust packing.

The next dilemma was how to turn the silver bars into convenient and viable currency. There was a great shortage of coinage in the colony, with most transactions being made by way of barter and trade, so Charles thought it fitting to mill the silver into a common form of currency called Spanish dollars. After some attempts, he managed to produce a satisfactory result and began circulating his new currency around town.

Unfortunately, this was considered counterfeiting and was gener-ally frowned upon by the authorities. It was soon brought to the attention of Governor Penn who, at the meeting of the Provincial Council held in Philadelphia on August 24, 1683, requested that a warrant be drawn to apprehend Charles Pickering on suspicion of "putting away bad money." Since there existed, as yet, no police or constable of any type in the village, or in all of the New World for that matter, a representative of the Governor was sent to fetch Pickering to the town hall.

Apparently, building and running a colony takes up a great deal of one's time, for Charles had not seen much of William since his return from the wilderness. As Charles approached the bench, he smiled at his old friend, now the Governor. Penn began to smile back, but then quickly stifled the reaction. Sitting up straighter and assuming a harsh glare, he spoke in an official tone, "Charles Pickering, thee are hereby charged with abuse to ye government in the coining of Spanish bits to the great damage and abuse to ye subjects thereof. What sayeth thee?"

Pickering readily admitted to putting off the new dollars but defended himself by stating, quite truthfully, that his silver was every bit as good as that used to make Spanish dollars and that the colony needed the currency. After supplying security for his appearance, Charles was allowed to go home.

An indictment was drawn up and presented. Counterfeiting being a "heinous and grievous crime," the trial was scheduled immediately for the following day. Charles pleaded "not guilty" to the charges, at which time the Attorney General called two witnesses, Caleb Pusey and Griffith Jones. Charles had paid Caleb £15 in new coins for supplies at the mercantile, which he produced for the court, and Griffith had borrowed £8 of the new currency from Pickering and attested to that fact. The Foreman of the Jury requested the names of everyone whom Pickering had paid with his new coinage, but to that Pickering refused, stating that he shall himself exchange any money he spent out and that no man should lose anything by him. The Jury was dismissed but returned soon with their verdict: "Guilty of ye Bill of Indictment."

Charles stood in Philadelphia's tiny town hall, beads of sweat futilely attempting to cool his body against the sweltering August heat as his old friend, Penn, read his sentence. "Charles Pickering, the court hath sentenced thee for the high misdemeanor whereof thou hast been found 'guilty' by the Country, that thou make full satisfaction in good and current pay to every person, that thou shall, within the ye space of one month, bring in any of this false base and counterfeit coin, which will tomorrow by proclamation be called in according to their respective proportions, and that the money brought in shall be melted into gross before returned to thee, and that thou shalt pay a fine of forty pounds into this court, towards ye building of a courthouse in this town and stand committed until paid, and afterwards find security for thy good aberrance."

That evening, Pickering was surprised to find the Governor at his door. "Charles, may we speaketh?" Charles nodded and ushered him into the small house, offering Penn his place by the fire. Penn greeted Mary before sitting down. When they were settled, the two men looked at each other for a moment before Penn broke the silence. "Thee putteth me in a lacking position today. Counterfeiting, Charles? What, pray tell, wast thee thinking?"

Charles shrugged his shoulders as he sat back in the wooden chair, "I knoweth not. Hath seemed a valorous idea at the time." Charles watched the stern countenance of the Governor gradually fade away until only his old friend, William, remained. Then, both men burst suddenly into deep laughter.

In the end, all it cost Charles was a fine of forty pounds sterling and the inconvenience, and small embarrassment, of rounding up and replacing his spent coin. It wasn't very difficult to do, as most of the coinage was still in his possession. Within a week, he made all of the necessary exchanges and went to see the Governor. The old friends paid a visit to the smithy, who smelted the coins in a ceramic crucible and poured the liquid silver into rough ingots, not nearly as smooth or as shiny as the original bars Pickering had received from England.

Luckily, Charles suffered no social condemnation for his acts and stayed in good standing within the community. He never did, however, return to his silver mine by the Pickering Creek. Mining the site would have taken commitment, capital, and equipment. Even though Penn's grant of land would have provided all the capital he would have needed for the venture, Charles' time in the wilderness taught him to appreciate the comforts of civilization. He decided, instead, to spend the next few years making a good living in Philadelphia practicing his profession as an attorney of law. He became so well respected that he was selected by his peers to represent Philadelphia County in the 1690 Assembly.

The New World had been a grand adventure, and Charles found his fortune, though not in the way originally planned. However, he grew anxious to get home, back to England. He was just thinking of how nice it would be to sit around a warm hearth and share tales of his exploits in the New World when the cold spray of another wave suddenly brought him back to the present. While lost in his thoughts, the clouds had thickened and now hid the moon that had been lighting the way, blackening the sky.

Charles shivered and began to turn away from the rail, heading for the companionway that led to the cabin he shared with other passengers, when, almost as an afterthought, he turned back and stepped up to the rail, climbing up just high enough to relieve himself over the edge of the boat. As he was wrapping things up, the bow cut into another wave, jarring the boat. The next few seconds were a panicked blur as Charles lost his footing and tumbled overboard, grasping desperately for some purchase before crashing headfirst into the sea.

Charles Pickering came up sputtering just in time to see the stern of the ship slip past him into the darkness. He tried to yell, but the cold water stole his breath. His heavy woolen clothes weighed him down, and an icy chill began to permeate his bones. He held no illusions as to his fate. No one saw him fall overboard; there would be no rescue. Before long, he lost sight of the lantern dangling from the forecastle. His final thoughts before he slipped forever beneath the cold waves were not of the land and creek in Pennsylvania that would for centuries bear his name, but of the green hills of Asmore, England, and of the friends and family that he would never see again, especially Mary.

Epilogue

Futhey and Cope, in their *History of Chester County*, note that Charles Pickering perished at sea on a voyage to England. However, no one knows for certain how he perished. No matter how he met his end, upon his death, the 5,368 acres of land Pickering obtained in America were divided among 16 friends, all men of wealth and influence in Philadelphia. At that time, his grant was designated the Pickering Tract, or the Mine Hole Tract, named for the operations he conducted there. Over time, the land came to be known as Charlestown Township. It was later subdivided into the Township of Schuylkill and the Borough of Phoenixville. Remnants of Charles Pickering's mining venture can still be seen on the land south of the Pickering Creek that also bears his name. The mines date from the 1680s and are over 300 years old.

One of the possible locations for Tinker's Cave, located off of Tinker's Hill Road just south of Pickering Creek.

~ Chapter Three ~

A Clash of Cultures:
The Tragic Tale of Indian Rock

Late September 1720: European immigration continues to increase. As they settle the area, Caucasians are gradually crowding out the indigenous natives who were once the sole inhabitants of the land.

A cold wind swept across the cliff face as the Indian made his way up the narrow, treacherous path that led from the river's edge to the high crag of rock that jutted out over the river, far below. The sun hid itself behind grey clouds, and what was a mild, sunny autumn day had suddenly become overcast and cold, as if the spirits were showing their sadness and displeasure. Below him, four white men stood on the footpath that ran along the river. They cackled with smiles of cruel anticipation, flashing crooked yellow teeth like so many demons sent to witness his shame. Their raucous laughter echoed up to him when his foot slipped on a slick stone, and he had to catch himself to keep from tumbling down the steep slope. He had come to hate these men, and himself, for what he had become. However, this had not always been the way of things.

His name was Alaenoh (ala-ee-no) and he was a Lenape brave, born in a little wigwam village along the very river he now climbed above. The white men called the Gans-howe-hanne the Schuylkill

River, but to Alaenoh it would always be Meneiunk, "the place where I drink." His village consisted of a few dozen wigwams, simple structures of bark tied to frames of bent green saplings, and stood just south of the mouth of the Pahkiomink, what the white men now called the Perkiomen Creek. His life as a child along the river seemed to him, now, like a faraway dream.

As he climbed the steep slope of the cliff, his mind wandered back to better days, when he was a child. The land on each side of the river had been covered with forests of great trees that the men cleared to create fields by setting fires at the bases of certain trees and chipping away at the charcoal that accumulated with their stone axes until the trees fell. In these clearings, the women of the tribe planted gardens of beans, corn, pumpkins, squash, and tobacco in the fertile soil. He remembered spending warm summers, as a very young child with his mother as she planted seeds and pulled weeds in these village fields. He remembered carrying water to the plants when the rains did not come.

As he got older, Alaenoh spent hot, sunny days playing at his tribe's fishing weirs. The weirs were traps for fish created by rings of sticks stuck firmly into the bottom of the river. On the upstream side of each corral was a "V" shaped opening that channeled large fish into the weir, where they became trapped and could be easily speared or netted. The village also had long dugout canoes that the men used to travel the river. While large and heavy on the shore, just two men could easily maneuver them in the water. He remembered how proud he was when he was finally old enough to join the men on their hunting and trading trips up and down the hanna (river).

As a young man, Alaenoh spent many of his days hunting in the forests with a hickory bow and cherry wood arrows, dressed only in a deerskin loincloth and knee-high moccasins, his hair shaped neatly into a round cap atop his head by using a clamshell to pull out the surrounding hair. Tall and well built, his skin bore tattoos of animals, his spirit guides, as well as symbols of strength, courage, and protection. One year, he followed the path that ran along the Gans-howe-hanne east, past the falls that gave it the name "noisy and rushing river," all the way to the village of Coaquanock. There he wondered at the strange village that the white men had created. They called it Philadelphia.

Each year, more and more white men came up the river and settled in the nearby hills. Once, one appeared in their village in the very midst of winter, during the time of a long freeze. The white man was obviously hungry and desperate for help. Manners and customs were of utmost importance to the Lenape people, so the stranger was welcomed into Alaenoh's family lodge without question and given his grandfather's place by the fire. At mealtime, the man was served the first cut of meat. The stranger stayed with Alaenoh's family for nearly a moon, probably saving his life. It was at that time that Alaenoh began to learn to speak English.

As more white men settled in the area, they cleared large swaths of land with big metal saws and built log cabins and homes of field-stone. They harnessed the water of the Sankanac, the French Creek, with large wooden wheels that powered mills to cut great logs into long flat boards or ground corn into flour. These men from across the big water hunted with guns in the forests and set traps in the streams until game became harder to come by for Alaenoh's people.

Soon, these new arrivals put up fences and created borders where none had been before. The Lenape were expected to respect these new boundaries that restricted the tribe's freedom to hunt where they were used to hunting. Many of the early treaties and land sales signed with the Europeans were, in the minds of his tribe's elders, more like leases. His people had no idea that land was something that could be sold. The land belonged to the Creator, and the Lenape people were only using it to shelter and feed their people. When the white men came and needed a place to live, his people shared the land with them, graciously. The white men gave a few gifts for his people's kindness in return; however, in the minds of the whites, these token gifts were actually the purchase price for the land. Yet, Alaenoh and the tribe tolerated the Europeans. In some cases, they were even friendly, greeting the white men with a loud "Itah!," roughly translated into English as, "Good be with you!"

Since Alaenoh spoke some English, he often was called upon to act as a translator for his people when they wished to trade or barter with the whites. It was in this capacity that he was invited to partake of the white man's firewater. He did not like the taste of the vile liquid, but manners dictated that he should finish what his hosts gave him. So, he did. The effects of the drink were not unpleasant, however. He remembers his father's disapproving gaze when he discovered that Alaenoh occasionally traded pelts for a bottle of the white man's alcohol at the trading place they called the Corner Stores.

Alaenoh soon found himself spending more and more time drinking. He lost his reputation as a strong and dependable hunter, along with the respect of his family and tribe. The liquor changed Alaenoh, making him rude when he was drunk and irritable when he was not. He did not have a squaw and lived alone in his own small wigwam. He knew his actions brought shame upon him; however, Alaenoh could not find the strength within himself to stop drinking. His traps empty, he had nothing that the whites would take in trade, but still he wanted... no, *needed*... more. That was how he had made the bargain with the men who now stood below, laughing at his disgrace. Alaenoh had agreed to jump from the cliff into the river three times in return for a single bottle of corn mash whisky.

Knowing him as a drunk, the men below saw in him the opportunity for some cheap entertainment.

Alaenoh had made the jump from the cliff into the river once before, but it was summertime then. Rains had made the water deeper, and he was much younger. Today, the jump seemed higher than he remembered, but he would not allow the men yelling at him from the river's edge see his fear. Instead, he mustered all his courage and ran, leaping from the edge, arms and legs pinwheeling in the air until he hit the water below with a cold, hard sting. He survived, and the cheers of the men gave him the courage to climb the cliff again. Perhaps the climb had taken its toll on his muscles or perhaps he was rushing to get it over with, but he did not jump out as far the second time. He landed in shallower water and hit the stony bottom with considerable force. He came up bleeding from several scrapes on his right side, but the adrenaline and cold water temporarily numbed him to the pain. The men showed no concern for his injuries and, instead, cheered him on even more. So, here he was, ascending the cliff to jump for the third time.

Exhaustion sobered him to the situation. The cold breeze chilled him, and he found his right hip aching and stiffening up from his impact with the bottom on his last jump. As he neared the top, he heard the men below yelling and hooting their encouragement. Alaenoh reflected on his past and the decisions that brought him to his current situation. What was he doing? Nothing was worth this jump. He should climb back down and ask the spirits to return his soul, the one he had traded in his quest for the firewater. He longed again for the days when he was a Lenape brave, a respected warrior, and the future of his people.

Allenoh stood at the edge of the precipice and looked down. The men yelled, but he could no longer hear them. His head, which had been spinning, suddenly cleared.

There was only one path for him now. He would not give the white men below the satisfaction of seeing him fail, laughing at him and taking from him the last of his honor and self-worth. He would jump, but no longer for their cursed firewater. He would jump to prove that he was a warrior, strong in his mind as well as his body.

Alaenoh took a few steps back, ran forward, then leaped off into the void with all his might. His mind was resolute, but his hip was stiff, sapped of its strength by the previous fall. He did not get the push off that he needed, and although he quickly realized that he was going to come up short and land in the shallows, he felt no fear. Alaenoh, warrior brave of the Lenape people, spread his arms proudly and looked out across the river as he fell, taking one last look at the land he called home.

Epilogue

"About halfway up the Black Rock is a crag which, at great height, juts far out over the towpath and the river beneath. Twenty years ago, it could only be approached by a long and difficult path among the rocks, rendered dangerous by steep descents and gloomy from the dense shade of pines that then covered the whole hill. A stunted cedar grew upon the very verge, and it made the most masculine heart tremble to stand upon the edge and, while clinging to this frail support, look down into the waters beneath. Sometime after the settlement, and when the simple natives had been in contact with the whites long enough to acquire their vices, an Indian was once tempted, with the promise of a bottle of whisky, to leap three times from this crag into the river. Twice he made the terrible plunge successfully and, returning after the second attempt, wearied with the wonted exertion and bleeding from wounds made by some sharp stones against which he had struck, he sprang again into the stream never more to reappear. Since that time, it has borne the name of Indian Rock."

- Annals of Phoenixville, Samuel Pennypacker, 1872

The author standing high atop Indian Rock (2020).

~ Chapter Four ~
Till the Cows Come Home:
The Tale of Lizzie Buckwalter

September 1746: Rural colonists are establishing the first farms, carving them out of the Pennsylvania wilderness.

Little Lizzie Buckwalter wasn't so little anymore. In just over a month, she would turn 10 years old... old enough to be sent out into the woods to herd in the cows all by herself and old enough to know when she was in a heap of trouble. It was summer, but she shivered in the cool evening air. Actually, the dropping temperature played only a small role in her involuntary trembling. What chilled her bones was the very real danger of being eaten... alive. A constant flow of tears cut tiny rivulets down the young girl's dirty cheeks, leaving shiny trails that glistened in the gathering gloom as she thought of what it would feel like *not to be* anymore and wondered how much it was going to hurt. She sniffled, smearing the tears across her face with the hem of her blue and white patterned dress, and began sobbing harder than before. As she fingered the woolen material, she thought of her father and brothers finding its tattered fragments scattered throughout the woods in the morning and saying to each other, "Poor, poor Lizzie. I'll miss her so, won't you?"

Elizabeth had three older brothers, John, Daniel, and David, who were all in their early 20s and enjoyed spoiling her. She also had five older sisters: Mary (19), Anny (17), Barbara (15), Susanna (13), and Laura (11). All in all, Lizzie's mother had nine children, one every two years, almost like clockwork, for nearly two decades before her luck finally ran out. She died trying to give birth to her tenth child, who would have been Lizzie's little brother. After the death of her little brother, Lizzie was doted on as the baby of the family, at least, that is, until her father remarried when she was six. *Now*, she had a stepmother and a little sister, Catherine, who was almost two. Naturally, Lizzie felt the jealousy common to the youngest with the arrival of a new sibling and the family's obvious shift in attention. And, as if that wasn't enough, there was *another* baby on the way. Her stepmother wasn't particularly mean to her, or to any of the stepchildren for that matter, but she didn't dote on any of them, either. She also never seemed to treat Lizzie like she was special. She wondered if her stepmother would even care if she never came home. "She'll probably be glad," thought Lizzie.

The twinge of anger towards her stepmother stiffened her resolve. "No sense sitting here and crying like a child," she thought. She took one last heavy sob, wiped her face, and stood up to take stock of her situation. It was just after supper when her stepmother had sent her into the woods around their family farm, in Charlestown, Pennsylvania, to herd in the cows. In those days, it was common practice to let the livestock wander free during the day, turned out to the woods to fend for themselves, and to bring them in at night, keeping them safe from the roving packs of wolves whose howls could often be heard echoing among the rolling hills. It was those wolves that Lizzie now feared as dusk fell around her.

Lizzie had been born and raised on the Buckwalter family farm, located just west of the Pickering Creek, off of an overgrown cart path that was occasionally referred to as Buckwalter Road. It was the first farm on the "Manovan Tract," the area that would one day become Phoenixville. Her grandfather, Francis Buckwalter, cut their family farm from the pristine Pennsylvania wilderness and, upon his death in 1723, passed the property on to his son, Johannes "John" Buckwalter, Lizzie's father. The nearest neighbors lived on the Starr and Coates Farms, several miles to the north. The Indians had farmed this land before them, to be sure, and at that moment, Lizzie would have welcomed the sight of a Lenape hunter with his deerskin moccasins and slender bow slung over his lean, bronze shoulders. The idea frightened, yet somehow fascinated her. However, the native's village was located a considerable distance downstream, where the Pickering Creek met the Schuylkill River, and by now, all the Indian hunters would be plenty warm while eating venison around the village fires, laughing with their families.

Lizzie had headed south into the woods after the cows. They usually did not stray very far, but on this occasion, they were nowhere to be found. Though getting more frustrated, she kept looking and listening until, at last, she heard the distant clang of a cowbell. Just over the next rise, she came across the first of the cows, standing in the lengthening shadows with its head hung low, nuzzling through the leaves. She broke a stick from a low hanging branch on a nearby tree, quickly stripped the leaves and little branches from it with her hand, and began the process of herding the cows together and getting them moving towards home.

Unfortunately, even with the slender green switch in her hand to persuade them, the chore proved easier said than done. The cows had spread themselves out over a fairly wide area, and, by the time she gathered them all together, the light was beginning to fail. Once she lost the sun, it wasn't long before she lost her direction, too. Lizzie started to panic as she realized that she wasn't going to make it home before dark.

The Buckwalter farm was located in an area originally called Upper Egypt, then Hardscrabble, and finally, Charlestown. Named for Charles Pickering, who first visited the area in the 1680s, Charlestown, to be clear, wasn't really a town at all. It was the name given to a few structures built around Job Harvey's Mill, located on a dirt track called Charlestown Road, which wound through a small stretch of backcountry in the very British Colony of Pennsylvania. Across Charlestown Road, Pikeland was still unbroken wilderness. Lizzie knew she was somewhere between that road and the farm, so she wasn't really lost. However, she knew she couldn't find her way home in the dark, either. Lizzy imagined menacing shapes lurking in the shadowy woods around her and wished for some sort of shelter, any sort of comfort, especially for that of her own warm bed at home.

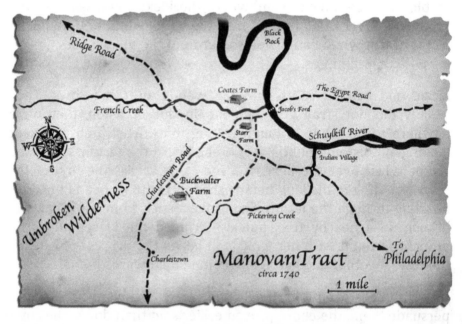

When he first came here, Charles Pickering built a small cave-like structure with a stone floor and an arched roof that was covered over with sod. It lay along the Pickering Creek, not far from her family's farm. Lizzie and her brothers and sisters knew the place well, as they liked to play inside it. The Buckwalter farmhouse, in comparison, consisted of a small cabin, built from logs notched and fitted together, with mud packing the crevices. It had one room with two doors to the outside, one in the front and one in the back. Inside, taking up an entire side of the cabin, was a huge fireplace with a great hearth big enough for logs so large they had to be dragged inside with a horse and took several days to burn completely away. Papa always called them *Yule logs*, even when it wasn't Christmas. The roof of the cabin was covered with shingles split from oak timber, and dirt was heaped up against the sides of the cabin to drain the rain away and prevent the water from leaking in. Wolves were so numerous near the farm that the sheepfold had to be built against the cabin and on winter mornings the snow around it would often be found beaten down by a pack's efforts to get in. If the wolves ever became too bold, though, a musket fired into the air was usually enough to disperse them for the night.

Now, the small old cabin belonged to her three brothers, for, when her father remarried, Lizzie's brothers built him a new, larger home out of thick, mill-cut planks as a wedding present. "I'm sure the thought that they might finally get their own place, devoid of the seven women folk, never even crossed their mind," she thought to herself sarcastically. The new house had two rooms on the ground level, a common room centered on a huge hearth, and a separate room for their parents, with an alcove for the baby. There was also a loft, accessible by a ladder, for her and her five older sisters. It wasn't very roomy and certainly lacked any sort of privacy, but Lizzie would have given up a week of dinners to be snug on the big down mattress with her sisters right now, fending off knees and elbows for sleeping space under the heavy quilted blanket.

A sudden howl broke out to her left, and Lizzie jumped with a start. She dropped the slender green switch and reached down to pick up a thicker stick off the forest floor. Then she backed against Bessie, the bell cow. The cows heard the howl, too, and immediately froze, staring wide-eyed into the gloom. Her worst fears were realized as the answering calls began echoing through the woods, at first from far off, then getting steadily closer. The wolves called to each other, gathering the pack to their newly discovered prey. The cows bellowed with fear in response to the predators' calls and instinctively closed ranks. Lizzie hung close to Bessie, in the center of the small herd, and listened with apprehension, as the wolves steadily closed in around them.

As the other cows pressed in close around her, Lizzie draped her arms over the bell cow's back to take the weight off her tired legs. She found the warmth of the large animal against her small, cold body reassuring. However, another howl, closer than before, quickly reminded her that her situation was dire. Lizzie whispered the Lord's Prayer into the old heifer's ear, laying her cheek against Bessie's neck. The words seemed to calm both girl and animal alike. Each Sunday, the Buckwalter family spent several hours in the common room, taking turns reading from Grandpa Francis' leather-bound Bible. Her grandfather was a Protestant refugee from Germany who suffered many persecutions in his homeland because of his faith. It was so bad that he was forced to read his Bible while stealthily concealed in a water trough. He finally fled his home, only to be pursued for three days by his own brothers, bent on killing him for turning his back on Catholicism. With some ingenuity and a good deal of luck, he was finally able to evade them by escaping to America in 1720. In November of that same year, Francis arranged the purchase of six hundred and fifty acres of land in the tolerant Quaker colony of Pennsylvania. There, he built the farm that Lizzie now called home, and he *never* took his freedom of religion for granted.

Lizzie abruptly stood up tall and looked about her. She had no idea what time it was, but the woods were pitch black beneath the thick canopy of leaves above. Had she fallen asleep? She could have sworn that she just heard a gunshot in the distance, and her hopes rose momentarily. Were they looking for her? After several breathless minutes straining her ears listening for another report, all she could hear was the moaning of the cows and her own heartbeat thumping in her ears. Her hopes fell lower than ever as she ultimately convinced herself that she had most likely fallen asleep and merely dreamt the whole thing. About her, she could hear the wolves circling beyond the herd, but they kept their distance and did not panic the small group. Most of the cows weighed 1,200 pounds or more, all could kick, and several had horns capable of goring and killing a wolf. However, large wolf packs could easily contain fifty wolves or more. Wolves were intelligent, patient predators that would not attack the herd haphazardly. Rather, they would circle and probe, seeking out the sickly and weak animals, the easy meals. A few of the heifers had calves, and Lizzie knew that they would be extremely vulnerable. But there was nothing that she could do for them now. Indeed, there was little she could do for herself.

The first attack came off to her left. Lizzie heard the wolves growl and snarl viciously as they snapped at some unlucky bovine. The cows shied away from the noise, pressing against her as they did. A loud thump followed by a sharp and sudden whelp signified that a hoof had found its mark, and the wolves backed off to regroup.

The canine predators attacked the small group several more times, nipping at hindquarters and soft bellies, but each time they were beaten back. The hooves and horns took their toll on the much smaller hunters. Each time they attacked, Lizzie was sure they would scatter the herd and leave her defenseless. Somehow, though, she managed to keep Bessie near the center of the group, and the wolves could not reach her. Finally, they succeeded in getting one of the calves away from its mother. Its screams echoed horribly through the dark forest as the wolves tore strips of flesh from the floundering animal. The cows panicked at the sound and quickly moved away through the darkness. Lizzie was so frightened that she could no longer voluntarily move her legs; however, she had a white-knuckle grip on Bessie's halter, and clinging to it, she half shuffled and was half-dragged as Bessie moved along with the herd.

The wolves were not at all satiated with the calf. In fact, the smell of blood only encouraged the pack. They focused their attention on another cow, somewhere close by in the darkness, harassing her until they managed to separate her from the group. When the heifer was thoroughly isolated, the slavering wolves overwhelmed her with sheer numbers and brought the animal down. Lizzie heard every bellow of fear and yelp of pain as the animal was ripped apart. It seemed to last forever. Inside, Lizzie prayed that the poor beast would just die. Finally, all she could hear were the wolves growling and snapping at each other as they fed on the carcass. She knew it was only a matter of time before she met a similar fate, and she did not want it to last long. "Please, God, I go willingly into your arms, just let it be *quick!*" she thought, over and over again.

The wolves were now completely focused on their kill. In the darkness, the alpha and beta wolves took their share, ripping away chunks of flesh and swallowing them whole, before allowing the others to feed. The rest of the pack waited their turn and no longer pursued the small herd as it slowly meandered away through the trees. Gradually, the sounds faded as they traveled over a small rise, leaving the pack of wolves behind. Lizzie had no idea what time it was, but she placed her best guess at about midnight. Her fears had not entirely disappeared, but they lessened. There were many long hours before the dawn, and the wolves may yet return.

Lizzie's little body shivered with the cold and as the adrenaline from the wolf attack drained from her system, she realized how desperately thirsty and tired she was. Her legs and feet felt numb. She thought about climbing on Bessie's back, thinking she might be able to lie forward and hug the animal for warmth and get a chance to rest. She tied the loose end of Bessie's lead to the nose-band on the opposite side of her halter in order to create reins with which to steer, but despite her best efforts, the heifer proved too large for Lizzie to get a leg up. "Just as well," she thought. Bessie was a calm animal, but there was no telling *what* she might do if Lizzie actually managed to get on her back. A rider would certainly be an uncomfortable feeling for a cow, and Bessie may very well bolt in an attempt to shake her off. Lizzie did not relish the thought of being knocked off by a low branch and left stranded in the woods all by herself for the rest of the night, especially with a pack of hungry, wild wolves not far off. "Well, hopefully not so hungry *now*," she thought in mock jest. Having no choice but to stay on her feet, she stumbled on blindly into the night.

The woodlands of Pennsylvania at night were a cacophony of sound. Crickets chirped at her feet, and owls hooted in the canopy. Occasionally, she heard the far-off howl of a wolf, but she was too exhausted to care. The cows were also in dire need of rest. Although they could doze for short periods while standing up, they were easily disturbed and could not sleep properly. At last, the wandering cows found a small hollow where no breeze blew. The ground here seemed slightly warmer, and the cows began to bed down. As Bessie eased her massive body to the ground, Lizzie snuggled into her and abruptly fell into a fitful sleep. She awoke several times to strange noises in the forest, but each time it was pitch black and, since Bessie hadn't stirred, she soon drifted back into her troubled dreams.

Lizzie opened her eyes and blinked. Dawn had come at last. She could finally see the outlines of the trees, logs, rocks, and bushes that had been such obstacles to her when hidden in the inky black of night. Lizzie stood up and stretched her weary body. A thin mist filled the hollow, and the world around her seemed somehow new and different from the one she had known the day before. The cows were lying all about, so she pulled a new switch and set about getting them on their feet. Though hungry, the morning brought with it all the hope she needed. She took Bessie by her lead and began climbing up the rise.

The soft illumination of the early dawn gradually gave way to a brighter light filtering through the leaves. Soon, Lizzie could discern the direction of the rising sun and, with that, she set a course northward and made for home. Along the way her stride grew more confident as did her demeanor. She had spent a night alone in the Pennsylvanian wilderness with no fire and no provisions, surrounded by dangers, and came through it in one piece. In her mind, something had changed. Soon, she stumbled upon one of the trails that led back to the farm and, not long after, saw her father walking on the path towards her.

Lizzie's father and brothers had been searching for her since first light, fearing the worst. He cried out to her and ran to her headlong through the trees. She, to his surprise, did not run to meet him in turn. Instead, Lizzie kept a steady, even pace in his direction. As he drew upon her, he stopped short and looked at her. She seemed taller to him, somehow, and although her hair was disheveled and her face dirty and smeared, he saw a strength and beauty he had never recognized in her before. Lizzie looked up at him with big brown eyes and said calmly, "Why the worried look, Pa? Can't you see I'm perfectly fine?"

"I can see that," her relieved father replied, and smiling from ear to ear, he scooped her up in his big arms and swung her around in circles, in a way he hadn't done in a long time. "*Too* long," she thought. Then, he hugged her to him so hard that the breath was forced from her lungs. At last, he set her down with a kiss on her head, and wiping a tear from his eye said, "Let's go home. Everyone has been mighty worried about you, Lizzie, especially your stepmother." Lizzie took her father's large, calloused hand in hers and led the way.

Little Lizzie Buckwalter wasn't very little anymore.

Epilogue

"On one occasion, the girl of John Buckwalter was sent for the cows and, after a long search, heard the sound of the bell at a great distance from her home. By the time she had collected the animals together it had grown dark, and becoming bewildered in the woods she lost her way. The wolves began to howl about her, the cows huddled together for mutual protection, and the terrified girl crept into the midst of the herd and lay all night safely beside the 'bell cow'."

- Annals of Phoenixville, Samuel Pennypacker, 1872

~ *Chapter Five* ~

The Redcoats Are Coming:
The Tale of Jonathan Coates

September 21st, 1777: The American Revolution is underway. Washington and his ragtag Continental Army have been forced into a deadly game of cat-and-mouse against the powerful British army.

Word had it that the British Army would be passing by, and young Jonathan Coates was determined not to miss the spectacle. He was perched high in a large maple tree, located on the edge of a field near his family's farm. From his perch, he had a good view of the dirt road below him. His father's map labeled it "The Great Road," but the locals usually called it "Nutt's Road" or "Nutt's Path to the Forge." Samuel Nutt was a well-known businessman who owned several iron works in the area. Jonathan knew that Nutt had paid workers to move countless trees, stumps, and rocks to create the narrow-rutted track that ran through woods past the meadows and farms. The tract connected Nutt's Valley Forge with another iron works located fifteen miles west, in Warwick. So, the road was also called "The Iron Road." No matter its name, Jonathan was in the perfect position on the road to view the British Army march and he was happy.

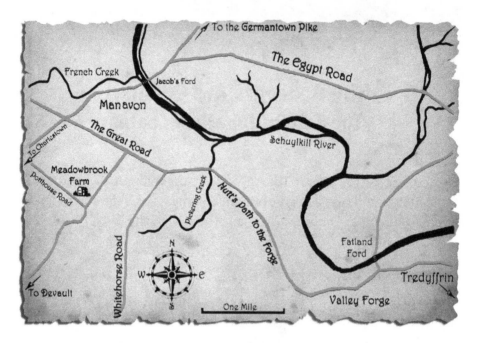

It was an exciting and frightening time to live in the American Colonies. British rule so discontented the colonists that representatives from each colony were sent to serve in a Continental Congress to air their grievances. Unfortunately, events in Boston Towne brought an end to any negotiations with King George III and Mother England. Last summer, when Jonathan was nine, the Declaration of Independence was signed in Philadelphia and open war with England ensued.

Their neighbor, Patrick Anderson, was a vocal patriot. Last year, Mr. Anderson raised a militia and rode off to serve in the Continental Army under His Excellency General George Washington. Despite his persuasive arguments, there were those among their neighbors who did not share Patrick's desire for independence from England. Many of the inhabitants of the Manovan Tract considered themselves loyal subjects to the Crown and their rebellious neighbors, traitors. Others were Quakers or Mennonites, whose religious principles prevented them from bearing arms. Then, there were those who simply wanted nothing to do with the conflict at all, desiring only to live and work in peace.

Jonathan's father, Moses Coates, refused Mr. Anderson's request to serve, claiming he fell in among the latter.

Jonathan heard the drums first. He adjusted his position among the branches in order to get his first glimpses of the soldiers marching. First came a vanguard of infantrymen in red coats, walking four abreast and twenty deep. Each one carried a musket over his shoulder. The dirt and grime of the march showed on their white cotton knee breeches and black leather boots as they marched by.

Next came the drummers themselves. Jonathan was surprised to see that they were boys not much older than himself. Immediately behind them came two flag bearers. He recognized one flag as the Royal Union flag, which most people called the Union Jack. The other was St. George's cross; red on white, it was the flag of England and King George the Third.

Jonathan remained concealed in his tree for the better part of an hour watching the troops march by. He saw regiments of infantrymen, grenadiers in bearskin caps, shiny brass field guns pulled by horses, and a squadron of mounted dragoons wearing long curved swords. While the British wore red coats and black tricornes, the Hessians, German auxiliaries paid by the British government, wore blue coats with red trim and tall pointy hats with shiny brass front plates upon their heads. The soldiers all looked healthy and well fed.

The sight of these British and Hessian soldiers contrasted sharply with the regiment of American militia who had passed along the same road only a week before. While word of General Washington's exploits in New York and New Jersey were common talk among the locals, the war always seemed like a far-off thing. That is, until ten days ago, when the ominous sounds of distant musket and cannon fire started echoing across the hills nearby. The sounds of the battle lasted most of that day. Some of the older men who had experienced the horrors of war met at the Lutheran church and began removing the pews in expectation of the wounded men who would surely arrive.

The American militiamen that came through a few days later were a rag-tag bunch dressed in rough, mismatched clothing. Some, lacking proper footwear, were forced to wrap their feet in rags. They were armed with muskets, but like their clothing, their firearms consisted of whatever they happened to have or find. The militiamen lacked any artillery and only numbered a hundred men or so. They came directly from battle, which had occurred on the banks of the Brandywine River, about 30 miles to the south. Jonathan bore witness to the groans of the wounded, as well as the blood dripping from the wagons carrying them. Some of the patriotic residents of the town appeared with casks of ready-made toddy that they dealt out to the militiamen as they passed. Compared to the Colonial militia, the British army seemed invincible. But no one greeted them with toddy.

Below, Jonathan watched as an officer on a majestic black stallion suddenly ordered the men to a halt. He shouted, "We shall encamp here! Englishmen shall occupy the north side of the road. Hessians shall settle the other. Troops, dismissed!"

With that, all hell seemingly broke loose. Men poured over the split rail fences into the fields all around him. Below him, several soldiers threw themselves down upon the ground and leaned their backs up against the wide trunk of the tree. Jonathan gave one a terrific shock as he dropped from a low limb to the ground right in front of him. The soldier started to cry out, then, seeing that the boy was not a threat, sat back and laughed, "You scared me right good, boy!" Jonathan quickly mumbled an apology before running off to tell his father that the Redcoats weren't just coming; it looked like they would be staying!

Jonathan ran across the wide, open meadow, jumping the small brook that crossed it. As he approached the farm, appropriately named Meadow Brook, he saw his family gathered outside. He rushed up and exclaimed, "Father, as we speak, the entire British Army is encamping all along Nutt's Path to the Forge. There's a lot of them, you should come see!"

Moses Coates looked at his son. "I am afraid we will all get a good look much sooner than you think, son." He pointed back the way Jonathan had just come. As he looked behind him, Jonathan could already see the blue coats of Hessian soldiers crossing the wide meadow towards their farm. "Come with me," his father said calmly, "we don't have much time."

Ever since the sounds of the battle on the Brandywine had reached them over a week ago, Jonathan's father had been making ready. Small valuables were secreted away under loose floorboards, while larger items were hidden behind a movable panel in the wall. Outside, wooden crates of potatoes, turnips, and beets were buried near the springhouse and behind the barn. All around the farm, items had been hidden away in case of just such an eventuality.

Still, there were many things on a farm that could not be concealed. The Coates family watched helplessly as small groups of opportunistic Hessian soldiers came in search of anything they could lay their hands on. Moses' primary concern was the safety of his family, particularly his wife and daughters, so he stayed with them. Jonathan was sent to find the officers' quarters and deliver a handwritten message from his father requesting a guard be sent to stop the looting of their farm. Jonathan hurried as best he could, but it was still well past dark before he returned to tell his father that the message had been delivered.

In the meantime, the soldiers emptied the gardens, the spring-houses, the woodpiles, and the barn. They took away the hay and straw to feed their horses or to use for their beds. The henhouse was cleared of chickens, and even the flock of geese by the pond was captured one by one and taken away. The last goose to remain was a fleet old gander, but unfortunately, he wasn't fast enough to evade a big, determined Hessian who finally ran the bird down. Grabbing it fiercely by its long slender neck, the man victoriously throttled his prey. When he looked up and saw the family quietly gathered on the porch of the house watching him, the huge man held the lifeless bird aloft and shouted to them, "Dis bees goot for the poor Hessian mans!"

One of Moses' daughters, Amelia, could take it no more. She rushed to the porch rail and shouted back, "I hope it chokes you to *death!*" Her mother grabbed her and pulled her back. The Hessian soldier yelled a curse at her in German, then turned and stomped off with the limp goose back across the meadow toward the Great Road.

The incursions continued throughout the night. When there was nothing left outside to take, the soldiers kicked in the door and ventured inside to see what they could find. Soon, the larder, pantry, and cellar were bare, but the family was left unmolested. Jonathan's mother and sisters were in tears, but his father remained stoic, reminding them, "Possessions and livestock can be replaced. Be strong and endure. Remember that the Lord looks over us. The safety of this family is our paramount concern."

When Jonathan finally returned home after delivering Mr. Coates' desperate plea for a guard, he was distraught to find the farm in such disarray. When he discovered that not only had the soldiers taken all of the livestock, but they had taken his horse as well, Jonathan Coates was heartbroken. The horse, an old gray mare with a black mane and distinctive black speckles on her hindquarters, was a birthday present from his grandfather just that summer. Jonathan tried to emulate his father's calm demeanor at the loss, but inside, he was seething.

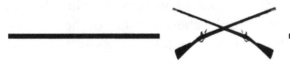

The next morning, a guard of four British Regulars arrived, finally, and stationed themselves around the house. The looting ceased. With the soldiers guarding the house, Moses Coates took his son aside. "Jonathan, I want you to go and check on the general welfare of our neighbors. Stay out of mischief and return by dusk." Jonathan promised he would be careful and strode off across the meadow in the direction of the Corner Stores.

As he passed the Anderson farm, he noticed that everything was eerily quiet. There were no people or animals to be seen. The farm seemed abandoned. Captain Patrick Anderson, of the Pennsylvania militia, was well known to the English, so it made sense that the Anderson family fled upon the arrival of the British Army. As Jonathan approached the house, he noticed that the front door was ajar and that the jam was in splinters. By the looks of things, the soldiers broke in and thoroughly ransacked every room. The windows were broken out, and the furniture was all smashed to pieces. A mirror lay in shards upon the floor, and a mangled painting upon the wall was slashed and torn.

When Jonathan saw the floor of the parlor, he started to panic. It was a bloody mess, and at first, he thought that the Andersons had been murdered. When he noticed the salt on the floor and examined the pile of entrails he found in the corner, it was with great relief that Jonathan pieced together that the soldiers must have butchered and salted the Anderson's cattle and sheep right there in the parlor, the best room in the house. Only one item remained in its place upon the wall, a portrait of George Washington.

Jonathan left the house and followed the small lane that ran down the hill from the Anderson farm. As he approached the Great Road, he saw that the soldiers had erected white canvas tents everywhere. Jonathan could smell the smoke from the cooking fires as the soldiers ate their breakfasts. Jonathan turned right when he reached Nutt's Road and walked the short distance to the intersection of the White Horse Road where John Longstreth had his general store.

As he came up to the front of the mercantile, Jonathan saw Solomon sitting on the porch shucking a bushel of corn. There were no free negroes in the neighborhood, but there were a few slaves like Solomon. While the old man was quiet and subservient to his master, he enjoyed the company of the neighborhood children, often entertaining them with stories. Jonathan rather liked Solomon. He seemed to know everything. As he walked over, Solomon looked up from his work and greeted Jonathan with a quiet hello. Jonathan asked Solomon what news he may have heard, and the old man said that he'd share, that is if Jonathan helped shuck the corn.

While they sat together removing the husks, Solomon began to talk and said, "The head of the column halted at the Charlestown Road."

"Where William Fussell lives!" Jonathan interjected.

"That is correct," Solomon continued. "The soldiers carried away whatever they could. In an attempt to save *something*, Mistress Fussell wrapped her bed curtains about her person and concealed them with her dress. However, her efforts were in vain. Some Hessian women accompanying the army had their suspicions aroused and threw the lady unceremoniously upon the floor, whereby they unwound the wrappings from about her body and made them their spoil."

Jonathan replied, "Imagine what a sight that must have been! At any other time, I am sure I would have found the entire affair to be most entertaining but, having our home stripped of our belongings as well, I find myself pitying her instead."

"As any compassionate young gentleman should," Solomon confirmed. "The army has ransacked every house in the neighborhood. Anything of value - clothing, provisions, even straw and hay - have been carried off. All livestock, including cattle and horses, have all been requisitioned."

"I know! In fact, they took *my* horse, Solomon. I reckon to get her back, though."

"That seems a tall order for such a small man, Master Jonathan. I am afraid it will prove a most difficult task. Are you certain you are up for the challenge?"

"I need only find out who is in charge. I can handle my affairs from there."

"I have heard that there are three Generals in this army, Master Jonathan. General Cornwallis is for the British, while a man named

Knyphausen commands the Hessians. Another General, named Howe, oversees them both."

"Where can I find General Cornwallis?" Jonathan inquired.

"I do not think you will be granted an audience with General Cornwallis, Jonathan. But not because you are a man yet grown, but because rumor has it that the General is indisposed due to bee stings."

"Bee stings?" Jonathan asked.

"It seems that Benjamin Boyer had covered his beehives with sheets and put them inside the house to keep them safe from the soldiers. Lord Cornwallis himself came to the house after it had been thoroughly stripped. The General inquired as to what was concealed there and was informed that they were bees. Not to be deceived by what he thought to be a subterfuge, the General apparently whipped off the sheets. Them bees were already stirred up from being moved, and they were just itching to get out and sting someone. Word has it his lordship beat a hasty retreat."

"Who would have thought that bees could accomplish what muskets could not!" Jonathan jibed, and they both laughed.

Solomon continued, "You can find the Hessian commander at the home of Frederick Buzzard, about midway between here and the Morris Woods."

"No, thank you. He would never do. Where would I find the Supreme Commanding Officer you mentioned?"

"They say Sir General William Howe prefers to make his headquarters around the middle of the column. Word had it he briefly considered the Bull Tavern, but since it only has two small rooms, Howe passed it off to his senior officers. Instead, he chose to make his lodging nearby at the Grimes' house." They had finished husking the corn, so Jonathan said thank you to Solomon and turned to leave. As he did, Solomon gave him a clandestine wink and nod, "Be careful, Young Master!"

Jonathan continued east along the great road, down the hill that led to the Pickering Creek, where a low wooden bridge crossed the stream. All along the road, soldiers had erected camp tents and sat around cooking fires. On the other side, Jonathan passed the Bull Tavern. Several horses were tied at the water trough outside, and soldiers loitered all about the building. He moved out of the way as a group of soldiers passed on the road, but no one gave Jonathan so much as a second glance. The next house was the Grimes' house where he hoped to find General Howe.

As Jonathan approached the fieldstone and thatch roof building, a guard outside stopped him. "Halt there, boy! Is this your residence?"

"No, sir," Jonathan answered. "Pardon me, but I've come to see the General."

The guard answered gruffly, "Go back to your home, boy. The General is not granting audiences today."

Jonathan conjured up his best version of his father's calm, authoritative demeanor, and standing up as tall as he could, he answered, "My good sir, I am a British citizen and have the full rights of any free-born Englishman. Those rights having been violated, I mean to speak with your commanding officer about reparations."

The guard looked down at Jonathan and laughed a hearty belly laugh. When he recovered, he said, "My, but aren't you the educated young master?"

"I do not intend to be rude, sir, and I understand that you are merely performing your duties. Let me be clear, though, that I am on particular business regarding my personal property. I require a word with General Howe."

"I admit you are surprisingly well-spoken and do not lack courage, boy. Still, I'd be flogged if I bothered the General for the likes of you. Scurry off and be gone!"

Jonathan tried one last time, "I defend my right to property, and you flat out deny me? Is it any surprise that the colonies cry out for liberty?"

The soldier did not reply. Jonathan stood his ground and stared at him with what he hoped was a stern glare. Eventually, however, he felt his resolve begin to crumble. Jonathan's eyes dropped slowly, and he turned, dejected, and started walking back towards the road. He just made it to the gate in the fieldstone wall when he heard the front door to the house open behind him. Jonathan turned to watch as a man with grey hair spoke to the guard. They were too far away to hear distinctly, but the gestures in Jonathan's direction were unmistakable. After a moment's conversation, the older man called out to him, "You, boy, come here!"

Jonathan turned and walked meekly back to the house. He tried to recoup the courage he felt just moments before, but it was like trying to hold on to a slippery fish. His father had told him to stay out of mischief. Needless to say, he would probably not have approved of Jonathan seeking out the Commander of the British Army. Jonathan began to feel apprehensive that he had over-stepped his bounds and was about to receive a stern reprimand.

When he got within a few steps, the older man looked down at him and said, "Private Wilson, here, tells me you desire an interview with the General."

Jonathan forced himself to look the man directly in the eyes and replied, "I did, sir, but was refused." After which, he gave a quick glance at Private Wilson.

"Please don't judge him too harshly. If he granted access to every citizen with a gripe, I would have no time to conduct the affairs of the army."

Just then Jonathan realized to whom he was speaking, and his courage began flooding back. He stood up straight, then bowed, "Sir General William Howe, I presume. I am Mr. Jonathan Coates. May I have a word, sir?"

Howe looked at Wilson, "You were correct, the boy is not deficient in manners or conduct." Then, he turned to Jonathan, "I am pleased to make your acquaintance, Mr. Jonathan Coates. Your refined demeanor presents as an unexpected surprise this far in the wilderness. I find it compels me to oblige you, sir. I was just about to sit down to a cup of tea. I would be most honored if you would join me, and we could speak of your purpose." He stood aside and motioned for Jonathan to enter. As he followed the General inside, Jonathan couldn't help but shoot Private Wilson a snide look of victory as he passed. Wilson rolled his eyes at the boy, in return.

Inside, Jonathan found himself in the common room, a fire crackling invitingly in the large, walk-in fireplace. The flames illuminated the beauty of the thick sycamore beams of the ceiling. A servant was placing scones and tea on the table where fine white china was already set. General Howe motioned Jonathan to a seat across from him. The tea was poured and they sipped it in silence, while Jonathan politely waited for the General to open the conversation.

"The weather is so much finer this week than last," remarked the General. "That storm was as fierce a squall as I have ever had the displeasure to endure in the field. So, Master Coates, how may I be of service?"

Jonathan set his cup gingerly into its matching saucer. He tried to speak as his father spoke, "With all due respect, your Lordship, I have come to air grievances concerning the actions of your soldiers. They came upon our farm last evening and began to pillage anything that they could carry off. By the time we were assigned a guard, my family was entirely divested of all our food stores, livestock, and valuables."

"I feared as much. All I have to say in answer is that the British army did not cross the Atlantic to oppress its citizens. We are disciplined professionals here to put down an uprising. My men are expected to follow orders. We are not here to break in doors, destroy property, rape, pillage, and burn. I do everything in my power to prevent atrocities such as those that your family endured."

Jonathan answered, "They were Hessian men, sir."

"Our German auxiliaries can be difficult to control. I do not deny that these unfortunate events you have just recounted probably did occur, but I have 14,000 men under my command. The pilfered provisions have likely all been consumed by now. It would be difficult if not impossible to determine exactly which soldiers were involved. Lacking any specific accusations, I am afraid that there is little I can do."

"You could reimburse us the cost of the stolen items," Jonathan suggested.

"If I paid reparations to every citizen who lodged such complaints, my coffers would be empty, and my army would soon be as penniless as Washington's. You must understand that."

"I did figure as much. However, they also took my horse. You don't eat horses, do you?" Jonathan asked.

The General answered, "I see where you are going with this, Jonathan. Was this your first horse?"

"She *is* my first horse," Jonathan answered indignantly, "a gift from my Grandsire for my tenth birthday, not three months past."

General Howe looked at him, studiously, before saying, "I understand. What if I told you that you could have your horse returned to you, or if he cannot be located, that I will provide you with an even better one. It would be a choice mount, I assure you."

"I would find that a most agreeable solution, General Howe, sir."

"In that case, I would like to make a proposal, one that stands to advance both our positions," the General added as he sipped his tea. "Surely an able young man such as yourself knows these hills better than anyone. I need to know what forces lay across the river. I would have you cross the Schuylkill and take an observation of the retreating enemy."

It did not take Jonathan long to answer, "General, no decent man would willingly commit espionage upon his neighbors."

The General set his cup down. He sat back, putting his fingertips together as he looked Jonathan over. He did nothing to try to conceal his disappointment. "By your manner of speech, I assumed you were a loyalist, like that aristocratic Judge I met over at Moore Hall. I did not take you for a patriot, young master Coates."

"I resent the accusation, General. My family and I, we are Quakers. Our religious commitments prevent us from bearing arms or taking sides."

"Your Samuel Nutt is a Quaker, yet he supports the independence of the colonies by making weapons for the Continental army."

"Mr. Nutt was a justice of the peace and a member of the Colonial Assembly," Jonathan answered.

"What, then, are your views on the current crisis, Master Coates?"

Jonathan thought for a moment. "Naturally, I believe it would have been best if conflict could have been avoided. My father says that the actions taken by our brethren in Boston were ill-judged and poorly timed. But, after what happened at Bunker Hill, any opportunity for peace without conflict has passed."

"I was at that battle, boy. It was actually upon Breed's Hill we fought. I personally lead the right wing of the attack. Our first two assaults were firmly repulsed by the colonial defenders, but our third assault gained the objective. The cost of the day's battle was appallingly heavy. Our casualties totaled more than 1,000 killed or wounded, the highest of any engagement of the war, thus far. It was a success too dearly bought."

There was a moment of silence. Then Jonathan said, "Only a few days ago, I bore witness to a noble exhibition of half-starved and three-quarter clothed men pass by along the Great Road. I had to admire how these valiant men of the Continental Army sacrificed so selflessly for congress and country."

Howe motioned to the servant to refill his teacup. "You mean to say 'For freedom against the tyranny of King George and his ruthless redcoats!' don't you?"

When Jonathan did not answer, the General continued, "Your true oppressors are those who sit and dine comfortably in Philadelphia while the penniless American militiaman is forced dine on his own shoe leather in the field or die. I know, from Continental soldiers who have crossed over into our ranks, that Washington's army is no more. Without provisions or pay, it is naught more than a mob and a rabble without discipline. They fight for unity, and yet, a civil war divides you. It has been over a year. Where is this promised independence? And, if we did leave, who would protect you, then? Washington has proven utterly incapable. To the west are tribes of wretched, wild Indians, who would descend upon you to rape, pillage, and burn."

Jonathan knew that threat to be false. "Maybe that was true during the French and Indian War, but that was before I was born. Very few Indians still live around here. After the war, strong anti-Indian sentiment caused most of them to leave. I remember a story about an old, worn-out brave and his squaw who refused to go. They bade their last farewells before seating themselves stoically upon a log where their own son dealt them deathblows from his tomahawk. Story has it that after he buried them, the whole tribe headed west, never to return. Of course, it's just a tale told in these parts. I can't vouch for how true it might be. "

Just then Private Wilson opened the door. "General, a detail has arrived with a prisoner." The General bade Jonathan to wait and stood up as his aide held open the General's long red coat for him. The general slipped into it and then went outside, closing the door behind him. Jonathan went to the open window to listen and see what was happening.

A soldier reported to the General, "A portion of the American forces were stationed on the high ground overlooking the ford to Quincyville. They were in an orchard by the road, enclosed by a wall of stone. It was a good defense against our musketry but provided little protection against artillery. So, we planted a battery on a hill opposite. It only took three shots before they abandoned their positions. We now control the ford."

"Very good," General Howe commented. "And who is this?" He motioned to the prisoner who stood between two guards. The man's clothes were disheveled, his hands tied behind his back. He had clearly been beaten. His left eye was swollen shut and his lip was still bleeding.

"Joseph Starr, sir, a local farmer. We apprehended him crossing the river, just downstream from the ford. He is charged with conveying intelligence to the Americans."

"What proof do you have, other than the fact that he was crossing the river?"

"Sir, this much I can confirm," the soldier continued, "We searched his home and found this document," as he handed the General a pamphlet. It was a copy of Thomas Paine's, "*The American Crisis.*"

The General handed it back to him, "Separatist propaganda. Burn it." Then he turned to Starr. "What have you to say for yourself, Mr. Starr?"

The man just stood there and said nothing for a moment. He then lifted his head and spoke, "I shall answer your accusation. America is my home. Yet, it seems that Mother England shall be satisfied with nothing less than the utter destruction of our American Liberties. Read the Declaration of Independence!"

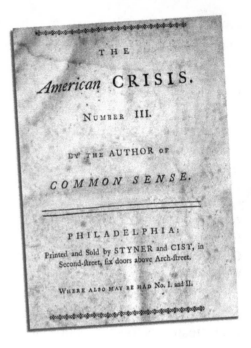

Howe looked at him, "I have read it. You downtrodden Yankee farmers believe you are doing no more than defending your homes. You complain of taxes, yet your taxes are now a hundredfold more than they were before the war. Your economy is in ruins. You have no imports or exports. Your larders are empty. Your officers are corrupt, seeking their own glory, and you, the good citizens of Pennsylvania, have all been misled. Do you not see that your 'Declaration of Independence' was nothing short of a declaration of war against the mother country?!"

Starr spoke again, fiercely, "Word of the atrocities you've committed precede you, General. Do you deny that, only a week ago, your soldiers massacred the unsuspecting men of the Pennsylvania regiment in Paoli, stabbing them to death as they slept? Those who managed to escape say you took no prisoners during the attack, instead stabbing or setting fire to those who attempted surrender. Have you no decency, sir? Have you never heard of the 'Laws of War'?!"

"Do not believe everything you hear, Mister Starr. Unfortunate atrocities happen in war, but contrary to your information, my commissary reports that we took 71 prisoners in Paoli. Moreover,

His Excellency, George the Third, has declared these colonies in rebellion, and as thus, traitors to the Crown, a charge that carries a maximum penalty of death by 'hanging, drawing, and quartering.' A most barbarous form of execution, wouldn't you agree, Mister Starr?"

James Starr just stood there and glared at the General.

"You are in luck, Mr. Starr. We shan't have any martyrs made this day. As this war draws to a conclusion, I look forward to a time when we can once again call ourselves brothers and sisters under one flag, the flag of his Majesty, King George the Third." He turned to an aide, "Colonel, be so kind as to read him the proclamation."

The Colonel stepped up, "Joseph Starr, you are free to continue your usual business, after first signing an oath confirming your loyalty to his Majesty, King George the Third. Upon signing, you shall be pardoned of all past allegiances, so long as you remain true to your oath. Do you agree?"

Reluctantly, James Starr nodded.

General Howe replied, "Very well." Then, he turned back to the Colonel and said, "If there is nothing more, I have matters of importance to conclude inside."

Jonathan was seated at the table again when the General returned and shut the door behind him. "You see, Mr. Coates, we are not barbarians. I seek only a swift end to this conflict for the good of all involved. Will you reconsider my proposition?"

"No, sir. I will act as neither spy nor scout for you."

"I respect your resolve, but since I indulged you, perhaps you will allow me one last point of clarification. Washington does not have the troops that he needs to defend the river. I flanked him on the Brandywine and crossed with ease. I will do the same here, tomorrow. As we speak, Washington is hurrying west in an effort to defend the Continental munitions and supply depot located in

Reading. He had no choice, really. This little war is already over; Washington just does not realize it, yet. That is why I will not pursue him into the wilderness. All I seek is to move into the city of Philadelphia where I will enjoy the winter months, in peace. Does that sound unreasonable?"

Jonathan admitted that it did not.

"Then, do me this courtesy," General Howe continued, "I will not only return you your horse, In addition, I will grant you six guineas in gold."

That was a considerable amount of money. Yet, Jonathan replied with indignation, "With respect, General Howe, I find it offensive that you think so little of me as to think you could bribe me to perform an act so base."

General Howe chuckled as he sat back in his chair, and said, "You are quite an unusual young man, Master Coates. I am as entertained by your wit as I am astounded by your audacity. Since you refuse to answer my purpose, you clearly leave me no choice."

Jonathan wasn't sure what the General was getting at and, again, he began to fear that he spoke too boldly. However, he sat stoically and forced himself to hold the older man's eye. "I will write you a pass permitting you to search through the camp for this speckled gray mare of yours. When you find it, take it home and tell your father of your adventures this day. But, retain the pass as evidence. Were you my son, I should scarce believe you."

Jonathan was at a loss for words. He waited patiently as the General wrote out the pass with a feathered quill. When the ink was dry, he handed it to Jonathan, standing up to say, "Good day to you, Master Coates."

Jonathan accepted the pass, put it in his pocket, and turned to leave. Before closing the door on his way out, he looked back around and said, "Thank you for the pass, General. It was a true kindness."

Once outside, the bright afternoon sun temporarily blinded him. He squinted and shielded his eyes with his hand. When he saw Private Wilson smiling at him, he waved bashfully before running off to find his horse.

Epilogue

"To the residence of Moses Coates, Jr., the Hessians came in droves as soon as the army halted, and they continued their incursions until the next morning, when a guard was obtained. The garden, cellar and larder were emptied and the hen roosts soon made desolate. Among other things carried away was a large flock of geese. The last of them, an old gander, was pursued through the yard and finally caught, around the neck, by a huge Hessian, who held the bird aloft as he throttled it and cried, exultingly, to the members of the family, "Dis bees goot for the poor Hessian mans." One of the daughters expressed the hope that it would choke him to death, upon which he began to curse and departed with his prey."

"The family of Patrick Anderson had been informed of their approach, and had removed and secreted as many things of value as possible. The bedding and clothing were locked up in the bureau drawers, and the house was abandoned. The English, who knew that Anderson was absent in the American army, broke open the doors of the dwelling and completely destroyed everything in it. They pushed the locks off from the bureau drawers and closets by thrusting their bayonets through the keyholes, and took possession of the contents. The furniture, which was in good condition, they broke into pieces and used for their fires. Mirrors were thrown upon the floor, and paintings and other articles of *vertu*, with the single rather remarkable exception of a portrait of George Washington, which was left in its place upon the wall, were ruined. The cattle and sheep were slaughtered, and the meat was salted and prepared for transportation in the parlor. The blood stains remaining after this butchery could be seen upon the floors when the house was removed in 1842."

"Lord Cornwallis came himself to the house of Benjamin Boyer after it had been thoroughly stripped. The beehives, for preservation, had been carried into a room in the west end of the house and covered over with sheets. Cornwallis inquired what was concealed there and was informed they were bees. Not to be deceived, however, by what he thought to be a subterfuge, with an impatient movement he removed the covering. The insects, already disturbed by their recent transportation, resented the interference by flying into his face and hair, and they probed him unmercifully."

"A horse, belonging to a son of Moses Coates, then quite a youth, was taken from the pasture field and it was known the animal was among the British forces. The young man went to the headquarters of the commanding general and, upon making inquiries of some of the attendants about that officer's person, received only insolent and taunting replies. He insisted, however, upon an interview with their superior, and was finally shown into Howe's presence. Upon making his errand known, he was treated politely and detained in conversation. The subject of the condition of the American army was adroitly introduced, and every effort made to elicit information from him. At length, Howe said to him that he could have his horse if he would go over the Schuylkill and learn, as accurately as he could, the number of Washington's troops. The offer was rejected, and Howe increased it by saying that he would not only return his horse, but would give him, in addition, six guineas in gold. The youth replied with indignation that he could not be bribed to perform an act so base, and, when it was found that he would not answer Howe's purposes, he was given permission to search for his horse through the camp and take it away."

- *Annals of Phoenixville,* Samuel Pennypacker, 1872

~ Chapter Six ~
The Road to Freedom:
The Tale of Deacon Armour

September 1845: Located just over the Mason-Dixon Line that separates the north from the south, Chester County is a battleground between abolitionists and slave catchers.

It was a bright autumn morning, and the leaves of the trees were in full display. Of the three men who rode north along the Hare's Hill Road, two were dressed unremarkably, which only made the third stand out even more. This man, in his thirties, was clad in fashionable Victorian attire, wearing a black tailcoat, red vest, and cravat tie, complete with a top hat. He pulled on a gold chain and removed a pocket watch from his waistcoat to check the time, before turning in his saddle towards his younger companions. "We made good time here from Lionville, but I'm not just paying you to guide me," he said with a distinct southern drawl. "After all, any educated gentleman can read a map. What I require is information. Tell me, what do I need to know about this man, Emmor Kimber?"

Abe and Cletus looked at each other as though trying to decide which one was going to respond. They were not as concerned with their appearances as their employer. Practical, wide-brimmed hats shadowed their unshaven faces, and they wore long coats suited for travel and outside work. Their well-worn clothing and boots were in stark contrast to the man in the black riding boots and high-waisted tan pants, who looked like he was on his way to a social event, save for the cavalry sabre on his hip and the two Aston model 1842 single-shot pistols, ready-to-fire, on his saddle.

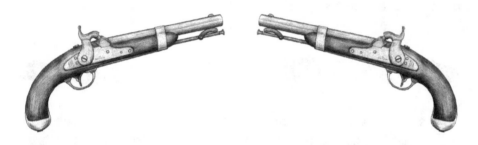

Cletus, the older of the two, finally replied, "Well, Mr. Richmond, Emmor Kimber is whatchya might call an upstandin' citizen, well known in these parts. They even named the village after him, callin' it Kimberton, which makes sense, I guess, supposin' as he owns practically the whole place, its general store, tavern, inn, grist mill, you name it. Best of all, he has this school there, just for girls."

His younger brother, Abe, broke in excitedly, "When we was younger, we used to ride out here just to get a gander at all them ladies dressed up in their tightly laced corsets and big, hooped petticoats."

Richmond continued to look straight ahead as he spoke with disdain, "Back home we call those skirts 'crinolines' and they are intended to keep a lady chaste by keeping men, especially men like you, at a safe distance. I highly doubt they could have been big enough."

Cletus concluded, "And, he's a Quaker, Kimber is. Like that potter, Vickers, we just come from."

"Another quaint member of the illustrious Religious Society of Friends, eh? Pacifism is undoubtedly one of the most impractical philosophies I have ever encountered," Richmond stated smugly.

"Pacifism?" Abe asked. He was almost twenty, just a few years younger than his brother.

Richmond responded, his chin in the air and a quizzical look upon his face, "It is the belief that any violence, including war, is unjustifiable under any circumstances and that all disputes should be settled by peaceful means."

Abe chuckled, "So we can push him around, and he won't fight back?"

"Theoretically," the southerner replied, "Although experience has shown me that humans are studies in contradictions. I can honestly say that I have never met a man who consistently acts in perfect accordance with his purported beliefs. Lucky for these Quakers, I am not here to test them on their convictions."

"Let *us* talk to Emmor Kimber," Abe laughed snidely, "We'd be happy to test his convictions!"

"Things will certainly go smoother if you simply let me do the talking," Richmond suggested. "In fact, let's keep your affiliation with the 'Gap Gang' under wraps, shall we? Your association has a reputation for general mayhem."

"Mayhem?" Cletus scoffed, "The Gap Gang helps keep the peace in these here parts! Why, we're slave catchers, just like you."

Abe chimed in, "Someone has got to catch all these fugitive darkies crossing our land. And, we get paid a good piece for every one we catch, too. We do a service!"

Richmond remained unimpressed. "You may see yourselves as avenging desperadoes, but word has it that you do not stop with runaways. Before I hired you, people told me that the Gap Gang is also known for kidnapping free Negroes and selling them off to southern plantation owners."

Cletus was unapologetic. "Maybe we do; maybe we don't. Sometimes, runaways be too hard to find. Anyways, ain't they all the same? One burr-head is as good as another. After all, they pay the same when they are on the block in Baltimore."

"Currency is indeed a wonderful thing," Richmond remarked. "All the same, I'd usually have steered clear of the likes of you boys, except that I was running short on time and needed help from those not just sympathetic to my cause, but also possessing knowledge of the area and its inhabitants, like you two."

Abe shifted excitedly in his saddle and pointed ahead. "That there is the boarding school, Mr. Richmond, up on your left. Chances are, that's where we'll find Kimber!"

Emmor Kimber was working in his study at the French Creek Boarding School. The morning light streamed in through the tall windows, illuminating bits of dust that lazily drifted through the sunbeams. The building was relatively quiet, as classes were in session. For seventy-five dollars each quarter, students received instruction in reading, writing, history, geography, arithmetic, astronomy, botany, cartography, chemistry, and of course, sewing. Students could also study classical arts and languages for an extra five-dollar fee. Down the hall, a student was softly playing Johann Sebastian Bach's Sonata No. 2 in A Minor on the violin.

The peaceful atmosphere was disturbed suddenly when a middle-aged woman, dressed in a plain green petticoat, burst in. "Fetch me, father, but thither is an urgent matter yond I fear requires thy attention."

Emmor Kimber looked up from his cluttered desk and answered, "Twilt be truly urgent for thee to leaveth thy students during class time."

Abigail's voice shook as she explained, "Three men on horseback hath't just arrived. Strangers, all."

Mr. Kimber tried to calm her, "Don't fret so, daughter, thee knoweth strangers in town art not unusual. Hath't those folk been directed to the tavern or inn?"

"Yond, I did," she confirmed, "yet, they remain in front of the school, demanding to talk to thee!"

The old man took a deep breath as he sat back and then reassured his daughter patiently, "Calm thyself, mine lief Abigail. We hath't anything to hide." He placed the quill in his hand by the inkwell and straightened his papers before placing his hands on the edge of the large walnut desk. Slowly, he pushed himself to his feet. "I will meet with them presently."

As Emmor Kimber pulled open the heavy front door, a middle-aged man with a well-trimmed mutton chop beard greeted him. The man bowed, removed his top hat, and spoke with a southern drawl, "Emmor Kimber, I presume. My name is Otis Richmond, and these here," Richmond motioned to the men behind him, still on their horses, "are my *temporary* business partners, Abe and Cletus Myers." The men did not tip their hats but remained motionless, scowling.

Kimber nodded but did not move from his place blocking the doorway. Nor, did he invite anyone inside. "Dost thou hath't an appointment, friend?" he asked, nonchalantly.

"Regrettably, no. While I hate to impose, I have been appointed as the legal agent in the recapturing of a certain group of Negro fugitives. A family, actually - a young buck, his mulatto wife, and their pickaninny child. They absconded from a plantation in southern Virginia a few weeks back. The buck, well, he is trained as a tanner, so he's more valuable than most and their master apparently had a liking for... well, let's just say, their owner wants them back. I know they crossed the Susquehanna River at the Conowingo Ferry, then made entrance into the borders of Pennsylvania. With the help of my local guides here, I have managed to track them north through Chester County, and now, the trail has led me here." Richmond pointed to the step at the old man's feet, then looked him dead in the eye. "In fact, I have heard it said that Emmor Kimber might be just the man that I need to help me."

Kimber responded humbly, "I am afraid thou hast been misled, friend. I knowest nothing about escaped slaves."

"It is well known that you are an abolitionist," Richmond stated.

Kimber stiffened, "Abolitionist is a term indiscriminately levied 'gainst any person who is't in any manner sympathetic with the anti-slavery movement. I am a Quaker, and as such, knowth in mine heart thither is something of God in everyone and that each human being is of unique worth. I valueth all people equally, and opposeth those who mayest harm or threaten those folk. So, aye, I believeth one person cannot ownest another." As an afterthought, he added, "Wherefore we hast did join and promote the free-produce movement yond boycotts slave maketh products."

"It is rumored that you do far more than boycott slave goods, Mr. Kimber. In fact, people have told me that you are a stationmaster on the Underground Railroad," Richmond stated coldly.

Kimber laughed nervously, averting his eyes. "True enough, friend, I am a stationmaster, but not on any railroad, above or below the ground. In fact, mine inn serves as our town's stagecoach station." Kimber pointed to the hotel across the street. "We giveth regularly scheduled transportation, three days a week, as far east as Philadelphia and as far west as Lancaster. Fare is merely one dollar and seventy-five cents, round trippeth!"

Otis Richmond's expression changed to one of disappointment and disdain as he looked at the top hat in his hand and continued calmly, "Unfortunately, sir, too often I have encountered men who professedly state that they obey the laws, but then secretly aid the bondman in his flight to freedom. We tracked these slaves to the potter, your fellow Quaker John Vickers in Lionville, then to here. Seems he has a secret compartment built into his wagon. What might you think that is for?" Richmond paused for an answer. When Emmor Kimber did not offer one, he continued pressing, "I even learned that you go so far as to call yourselves 'Friends of the Fugitive.' Well, may I remind you, 'friend', that *our* activities are being conducted within the limits of civil law?"

"A civil law yond maketh the north complicit in slavery by encouraging slave catchers, such as thy self, and coequal the kidnappings of free blacks, Mr. Richmond," Emmor Kimber replied impatiently. "Thou bringeth the evils of thy vile institution onto this valorous soil. While I admittedly regard thy actions hither as a serious violation of both mine constitutional guarantees and civil liberties, yond in nay way implicateth me in the harboring of fugitives, especially the ones thy seekth. If 't be true thou haveth any evidence ranker than hearsay, taketh thy case to the constable directly. Otherwise, I sayth 'Good day' to thee, sir!"

Before Emmor Kimber could close the door, Richmond stopped it with his boot and asked quietly, in a mocking voice, "One last question, friend; did they headth north?"

The old man's only reply was a gruff "Humph!" accompanied by a cross look as he closed the heavy oaken door firmly, latching it behind him.

Otis Richmond placed his hat gingerly upon his head and spun on the heels of his riding boots. Cletus asked, "You want us to go inside and persuade him to talk?"

Richmond shook his head and smiled as he placed his foot in the stirrup and swung himself up and into his saddle, "No need, boys. I already know everything we need to know. I'll fill you in as we ride." With that, he nudged his horse in a northerly direction and led them down the dirt track that served as Kimberton's main street. They turned right at a two-story fieldstone building with a sign that read "Chrisman's Mill," crossed over a little bridge, and then rode by a blacksmith's shop where an apprentice boy paused from chopping wood to watch them curiously as they rode past. There followed a few other assorted businesses, including a saddler and harness-maker, a shoemaker's shop, and a tailor's establishment. Before long, they climbed another small hill, and suddenly they were out of town. Richmond glanced back, "Charming little hamlet."

The Myers brothers rode up next to Richmond, and Abe asked, "What the hell happened back there?! I don't know what in hell he was sayin'!"

Richmond kept riding without turning to look at him and responded, "That was the King's English, my ignorant young friend. You'd have known what he was saying if you studied your King James Bible."

Cletus ignored him. "You saw how guilty he looked, Richmond. We had him dead to rights. You can't actually believe that those darkies ain't there!"

"Au contraire!" Richmond scolded him. "Our quarry *was* there, and quite recently, I assume, but they have since moved on, probably just within the last several hours. They are heading north as we speak."

Abe protested, "How can you be so sure 'bout that? They may still be back there. We never even looked around the place!"

Richmond explained, "There is no need to waste time conducting a futile search. While the village is small, there must be dozens of buildings back there and Kimber owns them all. Where would you start looking? Lucky for us, people are as easy to read as the weather, once you learn what to look for, not that I am confident that either of you would be up to the task. Kimber's body language told me he was lying and what precisely he was lying about, as did certain things he said and the ways that he said them. Tone and tenor are hard to keep under conscious control. In fact, they have the nasty habit of revealing our innermost secrets. One need only apply particular stressors and carefully observe the results."

"So, if you know he was harboring fugitives, we should have him arrested!"

"Patience, my dear Mr. Myers. One must choose his battles wisely. We lack evidence, though one should hardly require it. It is clear that strong men of conscience, like Vickers and Kimber, would never obey the behests of a law that commanded them to return human beings to bondage. These overly idealistic men actually believe that there should be no such thing as property in man. I am sure they would consider it performing their duty to conscience and to God when they help fugitives escape from servitude, no matter how misguided and illegal those actions may be. However, I am not here to battle these men. I am here to recover three particular escaped slaves and to return them to Virginia. And that is precisely what I intend to do."

They had not traveled far when a horse came galloping up the road behind them. The three riders turned upon the sound, and Richmond recognized the young man who had been chopping wood in front of the blacksmith's shop a short way back. The boy slowed his horse as he approached, but did not call out, waiting instead until he was close enough to be heard in a low voice. "If you men are who I think you are, I might know some things that would interest you."

"And who, pray tell, do you think we may be?" Richmond asked.

"Sl-slave catchers," the boy stammered, "I am thinking you all are slave catchers."

Otis Richmond looked the boy over before he spoke, "Son, I have travelled all the way from the great state of Virginia in pursuit of a group of particularly slippery fugitive Negroes. If you have information regarding their whereabouts, I would be greatly appreciative." With a gloved hand, he reached into a pocket on his waistcoat, pulled out a silver coin, and flashed it in the sun.

"Well, sir, I work at the smithy's in town. Being the apprentice there and all, I have to be up early to start the fires and get the forges hot. Well, this morning, before the dawn, I see that there is a wagon coming from the boarding school and when it goes by, I see that the driver is a free darkie they call 'Deacon Armour.' After seein' you all, I been thinkin' that maybe he's the one that got your slaves."

Richmond closed his hand around the coin and motioned as if to replace it in his pocket, "There seem to be many free Negroes this far north, all going about their daily business. What leads you to believe that this Deacon Armour is any different?"

The boy asked, "You ever heard of the expression, 'Birds of a feather flock together?'"

"Of course," Richmond replied.

"Well, these ain't birds of a feather, if you get my reasoning, sir. Emmor Kimber is a Quaker, but Deacon Armour preaches in a Baptist Church north of town. They ain't the same *at all*. So that's what got me to thinking, what business does a black Baptist preacher have at a white Quaker boarding school before the sun is even up?"

"I see your point," Richmond mused. "Tell me, what does this Deacon Armour look like? What was he driving?"

"He's an older man in his 50s, with a beard," the boy answered. "His hair is just startin' to go white. He was drivin' a red buckboard with yellow wagon wheels, pulled by an old gray mule."

"Thank you, you have done this southern gentleman a great service." With that, Richmond tossed him the coin. The boy caught it out of the air, looked at it in his palm, smiled, and then wheeled his horse and galloped back the way he came. Richmond checked the pocket watch he kept in his waistcoat, turned to the Myers brothers, and said, "Well boys, our quarry has a head start, but it is not yet nine. If they are traveling in a wagon, we should be able to catch up to them by early afternoon. The question is, where would they go from here? Come down from your horses and let us take a look at the map. A moment of strategizing will save us from haplessly flailing about, and time does seem to be of the essence if I am to secure my quarry before it is lost to me in the quagmire of the city."

"Their ultimate goal is likely Philadelphia," Abe answered, "but, that's on the other side of the Schuylkill River. There ain't but a few ways across. The main way, the one I would take, would be through Phoenixville, across Jacob's Ford. From there, I'd take the Egypt Road to Norristown, and from there it is only about six miles to the city."

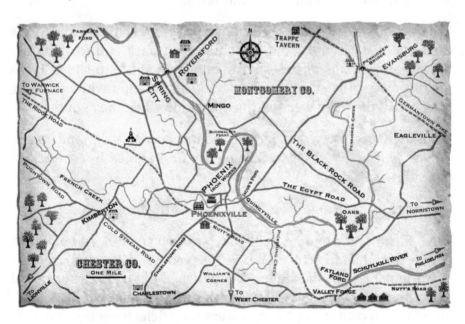

"Nah, I don't think they'd be goin' that way," Cletus argued. "Too many eyes. Not only would they have to go through town just as everybody is waking up, but Jacob's Ford is closed. They built a covered bridge across the river there just this past summer, and there's a toll. So it would be hard to just sneak across."

"Then they could have gone east on the great road into Valley Forge and crossed at the Fatland Ford," Abe pointed on the map, "and, from there, gained the Egypt Road to Norristown."

Cletus shook his head, "Wrong again, little brother. While that is the fastest way to Philadelphia, there is too much commerce along Nutt's Road. Authorities are on the lookout for groups of runaway slaves, and too many people would see you. If this Deacon Armour preaches out of a church on the north side of the French Creek, it would be my bet that he would stay on familiar ground. The next available crossing would be Buckwalter's Ferry at the Black Rock. From there, they could make for the Germantown Pike and follow that into Norristown."

Richmond said, "Tell me about this ferry."

"There's a landing built on each side of the river there, and the Buckwalter boys pull a flat-bottomed boat back and forth across the river by means of ropes strung up from shore to shore. If the fugitives went that way, it may have taken them a while to cross, 'specially if the ferry were on the other side when they got there."

"Sounds like a slow and tedious contrivance," Richmond noted, "which is exactly why it would be my first choice if I wanted to cross the river unnoticed."

"So, we ride north and try to catch them at the ferry?" asked Abe.

"No," Richmond pondered, "If they crossed before we got there, then it would be us who would be delayed. We follow your brother's original plan." Abe smiled and punched Cletus in the arm as if to say that he had known it the entire time. Richmond just shook his head and continued, "Since we are on official business and have nothing to hide, we will take the direct route through Phoenixville and across this new bridge of yours. Given that the fugitives are moving slower, have a longer distance to travel, and have the added delay of having to cross the river by ferry, I'd say we have a good chance of intercepting them somewhere on this road," Richmond looked down, pointing to the map, "before they get to the Perkiomen Bridge." The men nodded their approval. "We best get going then," Richmond ordered, folding the map and tucking it into the pocket of his waistcoat.

The ferry took the better part of the morning, but it was worth the extra time to ensure an inconspicuous crossing. Deacon Armour was a regular patron of the ferry and knew the Buckwalter boys well. All the same, he took a moment to thank God for their safe passage across the river. The sun was climbing into the sky, the morning chill disappearing with the last of the morning mist, and it was turning into a glorious fall day. The dirt track they were on wound its way north between farmers' fields and through small patches of woods on its way towards the Perkiomen Bridge Hotel.

Deacon Armour felt sympathy for Louis and his family, who had rode in a concealed compartment in the bottom of the wagon for several hours now. Once, the Deacon pulled the wagon into an isolated copse of trees to allow them a chance to breathe, stretch and relieve themselves. It was then that Deacon Armor got his first good look at his charges. Louis had been a tanner on a farm, and his young wife, Annie, was a servant on the neighboring planta-tion. Together they had a four-year-old little girl, whom they called Trinket. Annie could not bear the thought of her daughter endur-ing the yoke of slavery as she had, so she and Louis decided that their only choice was to run.

After several weeks of harrowing flight, Louis and his family were finally connected with an agent on the Underground Railroad. Deacon Armour wondered for a moment how that name came into being. He entertained himself with some ideas, but he had no way of knowing if any of them were correct. All he knew was that, for as long as he could remember, his family had been involved with the covert activity of aiding fugitive slaves. To his brothers and sisters in the movement, he was a 'conductor' because he accompanied the fugitives between 'stations,' or safe houses, along the route. Since it remained a federal crime to give aid to an escaped slave, the routes and stations were changed often in an attempt to remain unpredictable and to stay one step ahead of the slave catchers that plagued the region.

Soon, Deacon Armour thought, he and his charges would be on the Germantown Pike. From there it would be an easy ride to the Plymouth Friends Meeting House, where he would deliver the family into the safe arms of the Pennsylvania Anti-Slavery Society. There, they would receive new identities complete with forged papers that would allow them to once again ride in the sunshine of the Lord.

A small patch of trees shaded the road ahead. The foliage was turning glorious shades of red, orange, and golden yellow, and where they started to fall, leaves covered the road. It wasn't until he was fully under the shade of the trees that the Deacon saw the man on the horse waiting for him behind a tree by the side of the road, and of course, by then it was too late.

Otis Richmond calmly urged his horse forward, blocking the narrow road. In one hand he held one of the pistols he carried with him. The Deacon looked out of the corners of his eyes, but the trees he saw were blocking the sides of the road. There was just no way he'd be able to turn the wagon around quickly. Suddenly, Cletus and Abe appeared out of the shadows on either side of the narrow track, rifles in hand. Abe took the halter of the Deacon's mule, while Cletus leveled his rifle at the Deacon.

"Deacon Armour, I presume." Richmond's southern drawl was thick. "Let me introduce myself," he continued odiously, "I am Mr. Otis Richmond of Virginia. I have come all this way seeking one 'Deacon Armour.' Please, tell me you are him."

There was no use lying or trying to run, so the Deacon said a silent prayer to the Lord, sat up tall on the bench seat of his wagon, and looked Otis Richmond in the eye as he answered, "Yes, I am Deacon Armour. What is the meaning of this?"

"Sorry to inconvenience you, sir, but we'd like to search your wagon for a group of fugitive Negro slaves."

"I wouldn't know anything about that," the Deacon replied flatly.

Before the Deacon could protest, Cletus moved to the side of the wagon, reached underneath, and pulled the latch that was hidden there. A hinged board on the side of the wagon fell open, revealing a narrow secret compartment concealed under the false bottom of the wagon. "There you go, just like we found on Vicker's pottery wagon, Mr. Richmond."

Richmond smiled at the Deacon. "Clever design, but predictable. I'd recommend that you boys occasionally switch things up. Too bad you'll never get the chance."

Cletus peered into the dark recess under the wagon and could just make out several people pressing themselves against the far wall. "They're in here, boss!"

Richmond never broke eye contact with the Deacon, even when he addressed Cletus. "Get them out of there. They'll probably be thankful for some air. But be careful and get that buck shackled first."

"His name is Louis," the Deacon interjected.

Richmond cocked his head and his expression turned stern as he ordered, "Shackle *Louis* first, then collar his young crow and her niglet." Facing Louis, he said, "I must say, Louis, you are one inconvenient son-of-a-bitch, making me chase you all the way up here to Pennsylvania. Although, I admit that you must be either unbelievably clever or just incredibly lucky. I swore I had you half a dozen times between Virginia and here, only to find you were always one step ahead of me. Well, I'd say that your luck has finally run out. Wouldn't you agree, Louis? And, as for you, Deacon," Richmond turned his head back towards the head of the wagon, "what size manacles do you wear?"

"I am a free man!" the Deacon exclaimed.

"You *were* a free man," Richmond retorted. "That is, until you knowingly broke the law. According to the Fugitive Slave Act of 1793, it is a federal crime to give assistance to an escaped slave," Richmond added, waving his pistol at the three fugitives standing by the wagon, "yet alone *three*. Therefore, I hereby accuse you of being an active agent in the Underground Railroad movement, and I am taking you into custody."

"If that is God's will, His will be done. My angels, they watch over me."

"I wouldn't be so sure of that, Deacon. My companions, who are only with me on temporary business, mind you, happen to be affiliates of the Gap Gang. Have you heard of the Gap Gang, Deacon?"

"Yes," the Deacon answered, his voice full of disdain, "I've heard of the *Gap Gang*. They're a notorious band of land pirates, kidnappers, and slave traders. They *usually* conduct their raids down in south Lancaster, near the Gap Hills, from which they take their name."

"Then, you know that they don't shy away from kidnapping free darkies and selling them into slavery," Richmond taunted.

"If that is God's will, His will be done. My angels, they watch over me," came the Deacon's reply. His voice remained calm and steady.

For a moment longer, the two maintained eye contact, neither blinking, until, finally, Richmond looked away. "Chain up the Deacon and set him in the back of the wagon with the other three," he commanded.

When the prisoners were all secured, Cletus hitched his horse to the back of the wagon, then sat up front and took the reins. "So, which way do we go back?" he asked.

Abe answered from atop his mount, "If we take 'em back the way we came, over the bridge and through town, everybody is gonna see 'em, which'll lead to questions bein' asked."

Richmond nodded in agreement, "He's right. Although any white man here may arrest a Negro on suspicion of his being a slave, the accused is held in jail whilst the authorities confirm his identity. However, we don't have time for formalities. Our best option is to go back the same way the Deacon came in. We'll cross on the ferry, then back along the small roads north of town." He pulled out his gold pocket watch and checked the time. "If all goes well, we'll make Parkesburg by sundown."

After some difficulties, the Myers brothers finally got the wagon turned around, and the small party headed back down the dirt track towards the ferry. They had not travelled long when the Deacon spoke up, "Excuse me, Mr, ah... Richmond was it? I was hoping I might be able to ask you a question?"

Cletus snapped, "Shut up, you old coon. Nobody is talking to you!"

"No Cletus," Richmond intervened. "We cannot expect civility from the inferior races if we do not demonstrate it for them. We may not be equal, but we can still be civil." He slowed his mount until he was even with the side of the wagon, which brought him about eye level with the Deacon. "Ask your question," Richmond commanded, amused.

"Thank you for indulging me, Mr. Richmond," Deacon Armour answered. "I am a firm believer that you cannot critique a subject until you have examined it from all angles. If I may speak plainly, I can find blame for the attitudes of your partners in ignorance and poor upbringing. However, I was wondering how a man such as yourself, one who seems every bit the educated southern gentleman, can rationalize the actions you are committing at this very moment, right here, under this beautiful sky, upon these blessed children of God?"

The family of fugitives huddled close together in the wagon, fearful of the retribution which would surely follow such talk from a Negro to a white man, let alone a merciless slave catcher. "You just say the word, Mr. Richmond," Cletus called out again, "and I'll gag this smoked Irishman and stick him in the secret compartment under the wagon so he can't bother you no more."

Richmond shook his head and admonished, "You will do no such thing, Mr. Myers. After spending the last few days with you and your equally intellectual brother, I am starving for some worthwhile conversation." Then he turned back to the Deacon. "You ask how I can enact my God-given right to enslave an inferior race?"

The Deacon answered plainly, "God does not condone slavery."

"And yet there are no verses in the Bible that condemn it. Were there not slaves in the Old Testament?" Richmond asked. "Does the Bible not say that a runaway slave must be returned to his master?"

"There are other verses in that very same Bible that stand in stark contradiction, stating that the runaway slave should *not* be returned," the Deacon countered. "In fact, the entire spirit of Christianity and the teachings of Jesus himself run contrary to the idea that one human being could be owned and constrained by another."

Richmond countered, "The apostle, Paul, in Ephesians 6 wrote, 'Servants, be obedient to them that are your masters according to the flesh, with fear and trembling, in singleness of your heart, as unto Christ.'"

"Yes, if you read your Bible thinly, it may seem that God endorses the institution of slavery. Paul also writes on behalf of the runaway slave, Onesimus, however, in his letter to Philemon, 'I appeal to you for my son Onesimus, that you might receive him forever, no longer as a slave but more than a slave, a beloved brother, both in the flesh and in the Lord.'"

Hearing these words, the fugitive family looked up at Deacon Armour with deep reverence. Even Richmond looked mildly impressed. "You know your scripture, Deacon, I'll grant you that. But the laws of God are reflected in the just laws of men. Hierarchy and inequality are simply the way of the world and the way the world has always been. All the greatest civilizations in the world have depended on slavery for their growth and flourishing,"

"You mean like Rome, right?" Abe chimed in.

Richmond answered as though addressing a child, "Yes, Mr. Myers, like Rome. Why don't you keep quiet and let the men speak."

Cletus turned in his seat, "Men?! You forget that that there's a *nigger* you're talking to!"

Richmond snapped back, "You are the one who forgets yourself, Mr. Myers. Need I remind you that you and your brother are both under my employ and, as such, may be terminated without pay at my discretion, as per our contract."

Cletus turned back around, but offered a defense feebly over his shoulder, "We ain't never signed no contract with you."

"Then I suppose you should have," Richmond laughed. "Besides, the Deacon is obviously the exception, not the rule. I may even have a change of heart and keep him for myself as my manservant, my own personal valet. Would you like that, Deacon?"

"I fancy I should prefer my freedom, but if it is God's will, His will be done. My angels, they watch over me."

"I hope they will watch over me, as well, since our destinies shall henceforth forever be intertwined."

"I am sure they are looking over all of us, even as we speak," Deacon Armour reflected. There followed a moment of silence, broken only by a mourning dove cooing in the distance. The Deacon continued, "Is it not the cornerstone of southern political culture that our great American Republic is founded on personal freedoms?"

Richmond thought for a moment before he spoke. "Yes, that is true. But for social stability, freedom can only exist within the natural order. Science backs up the assertion that nature itself dictates that some people should be slaves, and some should be masters. For example, the brain of the average African is typically smaller than that of a white man, indicating that the instinctual qualities of the Negro are stronger than their inherent intellectual capabilities. That is why, intellectually, you consistently find yourself trailing behind your white brethren."

The Deacon motioned with his eyes to indicate the Myers brothers, then cocked his eyebrows as if to say, 'Really?' It took Richmond a second to realize the Deacon's meaning and another to ponder the situation before he smiled and said, "Point taken. Present company excluded."

Deacon Armour then pointed out, "If every slave-owning state has laws on the books forbidding the teaching of Negroes to read and write, then we can expect that their exercise of the English language will be less sophisticated than those who have been beneficiaries of education."

"Whites are naturally superior to Negroes and there is no point in wasting education on a working class," Richmond responded. "All you have to do is examine the reality of the situation with your own eyes. Whites are the masters. Darkies are the slaves. Since the world comes to us with this particular order, then anyone who attempts to overturn that order is doing violence to the world as God made it."

Deacon Armour rolled his eyes, "So, if for some reason the value of cotton collapsed and the millions of slaves that you say are part of the 'natural order' suddenly became an economic burden on their masters, how long would it take the slave owners to find out that the Bible was actually preaching emancipation all along?" the Deacon asked.

Richmond shrugged his shoulders, "I believe we need to recognize that people are capable of using whatever text they prefer, whatever interpretation they find favorable to their circumstances. If it is in our interest, rest assured we will find a way to believe that science and religion are on our side."

They were getting close to the river now. Ahead, the road ran through one last patch of brightly colored woods on its way down to the ferry landing. Before Richmond could ride off, the Deacon asked, "Might you be so charitable as to allow me to ask an additional question?"

"You might. To my surprise, I find myself challenged by your intellect, Deacon. Do you play chess? If not, I must teach you. It would be a most entertaining way to spend our evenings together once we get back home to civilized Virginia. What would you like to know?"

"I was wondering, sir, if you knew anything about the indigenous people who lived here before the arrival of the Europeans?" Deacon Armor asked.

"I am afraid that, on that topic, I know very little," Richmond admitted.

Deacon Armor continued, "Well, perhaps it was because he was not long out of Africa when he escaped north, but when my father first came here, he found shelter with the few Indians who still dwelt in these parts. They were a deeply just and spiritual people, and my father found common cause with them. In the time he lived with them, he learned their wisdom and their ways. Things like how to make medicine, how to fish, grow crops, and hunt like an Indian. To hunt with the bow, one had to get close to his prey, so they taught him their techniques for moving silently and remaining invisible. By the time I was born, the last of these regal people were forced to relinquish their ancestral lands and move west. However, when I was old enough, my father made sure to pass those skills on to me. When, in time, I was blessed with children of my own, I, in turn, passed these skills to my two sons."

"That was very thoughtful of you," Richmond commented. "Still, I'm not sure why you are telling me all this. Do get to your point."

The wagon was entering the woods now. It was not long to the ferry landing. "Yes sir, I reckon that we'll be getting to the point momentarily. I can feel my angels watching over us."

"Yes, yes, Deacon. God's angels are watching."

"Don't misunderstand me, Mr. Richmond. These are not God's angels I am referring to. After all, God has far greater concerns than the play we enact here today. First Timothy 5:8 says, 'But if any provide not for his own, and especially for those of his own house, he hath denied the faith and is worse than an infidel.' Therefore, I have my *own* angels."

Otis Richmond was becoming annoyed. He snapped, "You are boring me now, Deacon. I think I'll let the Myers brothers sell you south after all. It is going to be an unbearably long trip with you prattling on and on like this, now. Either call your angels forth or be done with it, old man!"

"I quite agree. We have reached a good place to let the curtain fall. But, before I do, I'd like to point out that, unlike my Quaker neighbors who tend to be pacifists, we free blacks tend to take a more radical approach to abolitionism." With that, Deacon Armor pressed his tongue to the roof of his mouth and whistled. The sound was followed by a second, softer whistle, which abruptly ended as an arrow sunk itself up to the fletching into Abe's neck. He didn't make a sound as he clutched for his throat. Then he slowly slid sideways and fell off his horse.

Cletus dropped the wagon reins and scrambled for his rifle, but before he could bring it to bear, a second arrow whistled its approach, coming to rest in his chest, just to the left of center. For a moment Cletus' eyes grew too large for his face as he slumped forward over the dashboard.

Richmond drew both his pistols and, using his legs to wheel his horse expertly, he searched the trees desperately for a target. As he was turning, a third arrow sailed out of the woods and planted itself squarely between his shoulder blades. His back arched spasmodically, before instinct, pain, and shock caused Richmond to drop his pistols and attempt to remove the arrow in his back. Just as he discovered it was beyond his reach, another arrow struck, not an inch from the first, and Otis Richmond dropped from his saddle.

Slowly, two teenage boys emerged like living shadows from amongst the trees. They were dressed like most farm boys, but carried Indian bows and wore quivers of arrows upon their backs. Deacon Armour stood in the back of his wagon and peered down at Otis Richmond, who looked up at him from where he fell. "Meet *my* angels, Mr. Richmond. This is my oldest, Bartholomew, and his younger brother, Charles. I'm afraid it would seem, sir, that God does not want me to spend the remainder of my evenings on this fine Earth serving and entertaining the likes of you."

Although in incredible pain, Richmond summoned the last of his strength and cried, "Good! You don't deserve my company, you filthy *nig-*" Before that final word left his lips, two more arrows buried themselves into Otis Richmond's chest. He looked down, as if in disbelief, then fell back and spoke no more.

Deacon Armour turned to his sons, "Well done, my dear boys. Killing should never be taken lightly. I am sorry you have to be involved in such atrocities, but such is our burden as warriors of God doing His will in a wicked world. Charles, run and see if the Buckwalter boys heard anything. Bartholomew, get me the keys to these chains!"

By the time Charles returned, Deacon Armor was helping Louis and his family back into the secret compartment under the wagon. He quietly reported to his father, "The ferry is on the other side of the river, Paw. They couldn't have seen anything."

"Good. Now boys, search them and their horses. Take anything of value they might have and put it in the compartment under the wagon. It will all go to support the anti-slavery cause. When you are done, take their bodies deep into the woods and hide where no one will come across you. Once it is dark, take the bodies down to old man Johnson's farm and feed them to the hogs. Toss whatever the hogs won't eat down the outhouse. Give the horses to Mr. Johnson, with our gratitude. He'll appreciate a new team come spring." With Louis and his family safely stowed away, Deacon

Armour, once again, closed the hinged board that concealed the compartment and secured it with the hidden latch.

Bartholomew asked, "What are you going to do now, Paw?"

"While you boys complete your tasks, I am going to take this wagon," he said, climbing up and settling into his seat, "and, God willing, finish escorting Mr. Louis and his fine family, Miss Annie and Little Miss Trinket, to our friends in Norristown. I am sure that they are quite exhausted by their arduous journey. They deserve to be shown some genuine Pennsylvania hospitality and to sleep tonight in the comfort of safety under the watchful eyes of the Lord. I imagine we'll all be making it home late tonight. I do hope your mama doesn't fret too much."

Charles worried, "But Paw, what if someone comes looking for these men and identifies their horses?"

"My sons...my angels...do not fret. God will look after *you*, but no one is ever going to come looking after *them*." In the distance, the mourning dove cooed again. Deacon Armour shook the reins, and the wagon started forward. "Be safe boys; I'll see you at home."

Epilogue

In Chester County during the 1840s and 1850s, abolitionists and slave catchers played a deadly game of cat and mouse. While the efforts of men like John Vickers and Emmor Kimber, both stationmasters on the Underground Railroad, are factual and well known, the character of Deacon Armour represents the many conductors whose names and sacrifices we will, unfortunately, never know. Otis Richmond is also a fictitious person, as are the Myers brothers. However, slave catchers like them, including the Gap Gang, were numerous and an unfortunate reality for those living in and around Phoenixville in the mid-1800s.

Historian Kellie Carter Jackson examines how Black abolitionists felt justified in resorting to violence to resist the unjust and inherently violent practice of racial slavery in his book, *Force and Freedom: Black Abolitionists and the Politics of Violence.*

~ Chapter Seven ~

Birth of a Legend:
The Tale of the Sundance Kid

July 1880: In the wake of the Civil War, the Phoenix Iron Works has made Phoenixville into a prosperous American town. While many young men call this place home, each with his unique fate, there is one in particular who is destined to live, and die, in infamy.

Twelve-year-old Harry Longabaugh slipped quietly out the back door of his home at 122 Jacobs Street. He made sure not to let the screen door slam lest he alert his mother, who'd surely ask to where he presumed he was going on a Saturday before promptly assigning him an afternoon of chores without so much as pausing for an answer.

Tucked into his waistband and hidden by his shirt was a 4-inch by 6-inch Beadle's Half-Dime Novel that Harry borrowed, without permission, from his brother Ellwood's room. Both his brothers, Ellwood and Harvey, went fishing for catfish down at the canal, earlier in the day. They usually brought back enough fish to feed the entire family. Harry loved catfish, but he hated fishing. He found it an incredibly boring task. However, like most boys, Harry did share his big brother's taste for fantastic stories. Harry especially liked the westerns, their tales of the frontier, the gold rush, and exploits of brave cowboys battling savage Indians, the likes of which hadn't been seen in this neck of the woods for over a hundred years. His mother tolerated his older brother reading such things, but forbade it of young Harry, whom she considered far too impressionable.

Harry was about to cut across the yard to the garden to grab a ripe tomato when the smell of pipe tobacco wafting by on the soft breeze froze him in his tracks. He cringed as he thought he escaped his mother only to get caught by his father, who would surely also have plenty of chores for him to do. Suddenly, he heard his father's voice coming from the yard next door. "We fought a revolution to free ourselves of the yoke, yet it seems some would wear it with pride!" his father complained to their neighbor. "Folks like Whitaker make a fortune on the lives of the working man, yet *now* we should name our town after him? The devil has a special little place in hell reserved for powerful men who get rich on the sweat and toil of the downtrodden."

Most folks in town would tell you that they lived in Quincyville, and they would be correct. Recently though, more and more people were referring to the little village on the Schuylkill River as Mont Clare, which was the name of the Whitaker estate. Joseph Whitaker was, at that time at least, the hamlet's best-known resident. Formerly an ironmaster of the Phoenix Iron Works, he obtained a charter in the 1840s to build the covered toll bridge that spanned the river over Jacob's Ford. Soon after, Whitaker retired and moved across the river where he built a new home and a steam-powered sawmill, which Harry had to admit was pretty neat. Whitaker called his estate Mont Clare, and some must've thought that sounded a sight fancier than Quincyville for now they aimed to rename the town. However, many regular folks like Harry's father didn't take kindly to naming the town after a rich man, not when one considered that he made his money on the backs of the workers at the Iron Mill, mostly immigrants and freed slaves from the south, who worked long hours for low pay in extremely dangerous conditions.

Whatever the name, the small cluster of buildings by the river was Harry's home and he knew every inch like the back of his hand. Aside from Whitaker's sawmill, there were almost thirty houses, a tavern, inn, general store, and lumberyard. There used to be an iron foundry and machine shop, as well, but they had recently been converted into a paper mill. There was also a post office, but that had been closed since Harry was a baby. Wagons paid their toll to clatter across the covered bridge to and from Phoenixville as mules pulled barges along the canal on the towpath below.

Completed in the 1820s, the Oakes Reach Canal of the Schuylkill Navigation System began at Lock 60, near Harry's house, ran down past neighboring Port Providence, and reentered the river at Oaks. The Black Rock Dam was built upriver to create a slack-water pool that made for great swimming, but what really excited Harry was the railroad.

Harry knew all about the railroads. The Pennsylvania Railroad's Schuylkill branch was currently being constructed to compete with the already well-established P&R Railroad. The tracks crossed the river on a very high bridge, almost a stone's throw from Harry's house. Newly constructed, Harry watched with childhood fascination for nearly a year  taller and taller each day, until eventually it towered over everything in town. Across the river, the rails passed along the north side of the Phoenix Iron Works, beyond which the line split. The main fork would eventually go all the way to Reading, but before it could do that, a tunnel would have to be dug through Fairview Hill on the north side of town. The other fork would continue along the Pickering Creek Valley to connect with the Main Line at Paoli.

The Philadelphia and Reading Railroad (P&R) was one of the first railroads constructed in the United States and had served Phoenixville since its completion in 1843. Constructed to haul anthracite coal from the mines in Pottsville to Reading and then onward to Philadelphia, it followed the gently graded banks of the Schuylkill River for nearly its entire 93-mile journey. The P&R's main line entered the east side of town at the Columbia Station, above Bridge Street, and passed under the north side of town, through the Black Rock Tunnel on its way to Reading.

Harry knew about the tunnel, too. Once, when he and a friend were cutting through it to climb Indian Rock which lay on the other side, they met a man who worked for the railroad. The man was a track inspector who walked the line with a little trolley on wheels that he pushed along with a short handle. The trolley had a little mirror on it that allowed the lineman to check under the rails for cracks and stress fractures. If one were found, the lineman shut down the track, and the rail had to be replaced before another train could come through. The man welcomed the boys' company and told them that the tunnel, opened in 1838, was only the second rail tunnel constructed in the United States and was just shy of 2,000 feet long. He also said that a local miner, Charles Wheatley, examined the rock excavated from the tunnel and identified many previously unknown fossilized species, some of which now bore his name. Harry looked for some of those fossils once but gave up after only a short while. Fossil hunting, he quickly decided, reminded him too much of fishing.

Having successfully avoided his father, Harry walked quickly to the mouth of the covered bridge. He greeted Thomas, the toll keeper, then started across as there was no toll for foot traffic. Once on the other side, he took a sharp right and climbed the embankment to the P&R tracks. A short way up, they crossed the French Creek, but just before he got there, Harry took a little footpath that led him down to the bank of the creek. There, he found a quiet, mossy spot to sit, pulled out his brother's half-dime novel, and set about the busy afternoon he had planned for himself, reading. Perhaps later he would also take a swim.

The half-dime novel was a Western. Harry had his eyes on it for weeks before a chance came for him to get it from Ellwood and he could find a place to be away from everyone long enough to read it. At 100 pages, Harry figured it would take most of the afternoon, and he dived in with zest.

First, Harry read about William Frederick Cody, who got his nickname "Buffalo Bill" after the American Civil War, when he had a contract to supply Kansas Pacific Railroad workers with buffalo meat. Cody earned the nickname by killing 4,280 buffalo in eighteen months during 1867–1868. As it turned out, another man, named Bill Comstock, also wanted to be called Buffalo Bill, so Cody and Comstock competed in a buffalo-shooting match over the exclusive right

to use the name. Cody won by killing 69 bison to Comstock's 48. Harry read that, when they shot all those buffalo, many of them just laid out in the sun to rot. That seemed like such a waste to Harry. Why kill them if you weren't going to eat them? He figured the buzzards didn't mind, though, and he imagined they must've gotten so fat on buffalo that they couldn't fly anymore. The thought of all those buzzards flapping around like a bunch of chickens got him laughing out loud to himself.

The next story was better. It told about how the James brothers joined with Cole Younger and other former Confederates to form the James-Younger Gang. With Jesse James as the public face of the gang, they succeeded in carrying out a string of robberies from Iowa to Texas and from Kansas to West Virginia. They robbed banks, stagecoaches, and even a fair in Kansas City. The robberies often took place in front of large crowds with Jesse hamming it up for the bystanders.

On July 21, 1873, the James Younger Gang turned to train robbery, derailing the Rock Island train in Adair, Iowa, and stealing approximately $3,000. The book said that the gang robbed passengers in only two train hold-ups since Jesse James typically limited his gang's raiding to the express safe in the baggage car. The story gave Jesse James an almost Robin Hood-like image that stirred Harry's soul.

As the afternoon wore on, Harry read the rest of the novel, but his mind kept returning to the image of Jesse James. He wished he could stay longer, but if he didn't get home before Ellwood and Harvey, he'd have a heck of a time sneaking the book back. As he climbed the embankment to the tracks, Harry heard the whistle of the steam engine sounding its approach to the station. He stepped clear of the tracks and was about to make his way down to Bridge Street when he got an idea.

Harry ducked under some brush near the track and waited for the train. It wasn't long before the large steam locomotive chugged into view, billowing white smoke from its furnace and steam from its boiler. The brakes squealed, and the couplings clanged as the cars slowed down for a stop at the station up ahead. As the clack of the wheels on the track slowed, Harry saw his opportunity.

The train had just about stopped when a boxcar came along with an open door. Harry dashed out from his hiding spot and jumped for the opening as it went by. Heaving himself aboard, Harry quickly rolled to his feet, pulled index finger revolvers from invisible holsters on his imaginary gun belt, and shouted into the darkness, "Freeze, ya varmints! I'm the dreaded outlaw, Handsome Harry, and this here is a hold-up!"

Three years later, at the age of 15, Harry Alonzo Longabaugh left his family home in Mont Clare and traveled westward on a covered wagon with his cousin, George. Seven years after that, in 1887, Harry stole a gun, horse, and saddle from a ranch in Sundance, Wyoming. While attempting to flee, he was captured by authorities, convicted, and sentenced to 18 months in jail. During his jail time, Harry adopted the nickname the "Sundance Kid." He went on to become an outlaw and member of Butch Cassidy's Wild Bunch gang. Together they committed the longest string of successful train and bank robberies in American history. The Wild Bunch gang claimed to make every attempt to abstain from killing people and although the Sundance Kid was reportedly fast with a gun and often referred to as a "gunfighter," Harry is not known to have killed anyone prior to a later shootout in Bolivia, where he and Butch Cassidy were alleged to have been killed.

The Wild Bunch Gang
Fort Worth, Texas, 1900

Sitting (left to right): Harry A. Longabaugh (the Sundance Kid), Ben Kilpatrick, (the Tall Texan), Robert Leroy Parker (Butch Cassidy). **Standing (left to right):** Will Carver (News Carver), Harvey Logan (Kid Curry).

Epilogue

In 2017, *Town Trekkers*, a show that explores the history of small towns, produced an episode about Harry Longabaugh, aka the Sundance Kid, and his childhood growing up in Phoenixville and Mont Clare. Their investigation uncovered an exciting and unexpected discovery in the Morris Cemetery.

A 3-D ground-penetrating radar scan revealed a mysterious coffin-shaped mass buried alongside the coffins of the Sundance Kid's family, in a location where there is no record of a body ever being interred.

Closer examination confirmed that the unidentified object was, in fact, buried approximately two feet deeper than the coffins beside it. "If a famous person was buried at that time, they'd often be buried deeper than the usual six-feet as a deterrent against grave robbers," remarked Ryan Conroy, then President of the Phoenixville Historical Society.

While his infamous exploits with Butch Cassidy and the Wild Bunch took place west of the Mississippi, Longabaugh apparently kept in touch with his loved ones in Phoenixville, making several clandestine trips back east to visit his family.

Historians disagree on how Harry Longabaugh met his end. Many believe that Harry and Butch died in a shootout with authorities in Bolivia, after fleeing the United States. However, recent DNA testing has revealed that the body buried in what was thought to be the Sundance Kid's grave is not the body of Harry Longabaugh.

It stands to reason that Harry may have secretly returned home, lived out his remaining days in peaceful obscurity, and was secretly buried in the family plot after his death.

~ Chapter Eight ~
Escape at the Colonial:
The Tale of the Great Houdini

January 2nd, 1917: New technologies, such as electricity and automobiles, are beginning to change the world. Yet, though innovations like silent movies are becoming more and more popular, vaudeville is still the king of entertainment. And what's more, the biggest box office star in vaudeville is coming to Phoenixville... for one magical night only... at the Colonial.

Wilhelmina Beatrice Rahner, better known as Bess Houdini, refused to make eye contact with her husband when she was perturbed. He loved her like no other, but the habit irked him to no end. The couple had hardly spoken since the train pulled out of Philadelphia's 30th Street Station, nearly an hour ago.

Finally, Bess could take it no more. Without taking her gaze from the Pennsylvania countryside sliding by her outside the train window, she broke the silence, "Harry, I don't understand how you plan to escape from a safe that you will barely have time to examine, let alone rig. I know you don't want to hear this, but... what if you can't do it? At the very least, it would ruin your reputation. And, at very worst, you... you would..." Her voice trailed off as she shook her head as though to drive the thought from her mind, and then continued plaintively, "Why not just do the milk can escape?"

"Worry not, fair maiden," Harry answered dramatically, in an obvious attempt to melt her frozen countenance. "'Tis the beginning of a new year," he continued, unrattled by his wife's concern. "Mark my words, my good lady, 1917 will be a year of *wonders*. Let this little escapade hereby be the first!"

"You clown now, but one of these days you are going to push your luck too far and make me into a lonely widow... or, maybe *not* so lonely," she teased, glancing at him subtly out of the corner of her eye to take in his reaction. She was quite pleased to see him furrow his brow as he did a double-take.

He rallied quickly, though, "It is not death that a man should fear, but he should fear never beginning to live. Marcus Aurelius."

"My dear, you've already lived enough life for ten men," she said quietly, her mood softening. "What is the name of the next town again?"

"Phoenixville, named for the bird. It's a steel town, about halfway to Reading. Richard reports that they have a good theater for a small town. Speaking of which," he checked his pocket watch, "we should be pulling into the station within a few minutes. Richard will be there to greet us, with the local constable. It's almost time to set the hook." Harry grinned.

Despite the cold January morning, the platform was packed with excited spectators as the train steamed into the Columbia Station. All talking ceased with the squealing of the brakes as the engineer pulled on the lever that directed the boiler pressure to the brake blocks on the locomotive wheels. Slowly, the huge steam engine ground to a halt.

An anxious silence fell over the expectant crowd as a pair of sharply dressed conductors stepped up and opened the wooden sliding doors of the passenger car. At first, nothing happened.

Then, a sudden cry of excitement arose as the one and only Harry Houdini dramatically exited the car, waving his hands high.

Not far away, he spied his road manager, Richard, standing on a low platform along with a burly man wearing a blue police uniform and hat. Harry shook people's hands and returned their greetings as he made his way slowly through the crowd over to the makeshift stage. It was made up of two planks laid simply across a pair of empty packing crates.

Richard offered him a hand up, "Hello, Harry! Let me introduce you to Captain Gill, Phoenixville's chief of police. Captain Gill, it is my distinct pleasure to introduce to you, the Great Houdini!"

Harry smiled and shook the man's bear paw of a hand, "Pleasure to meet you, Captain. I trust you brought the goods?"

"Indeed, I did," the burly man answered, producing a pair of heavy handcuffs. "I hope you are as good as you say. I'd hate to embarrass you in front of all these fine people."

"On the contrary, sir, if there is humble pie to be had, let it be my honor to serve you up a generous slice. Would you do the honors?" With that, Houdini removed his jacket, handed it to Richard, and then pulled up the sleeves of his wool shirt, presenting his bare wrists to the officer.

As the crowd watched in suspense, Captain Gill slipped an iron manacle onto each of Harry's wrists. He then locked each one separately by inserting a long key into the end of a lock cylinder and turning it five times in order to firmly anchor the locking pin. Captain Gill smiled proudly when he was finished and said, "Good luck, Mr. Houdini. You're going to need it, I'm afraid." He then stepped down to enjoy the show.

Harry raised his arms to present his cuffed hands to the assembled crowd. His wrists were now connected to each other by three links of heavy chain. Then he lowered his arms, keeping them extended, while Richard placed Harry's coat over his hands. Only a few seconds went by before someone in the audience protested the action, yelling, "Hey, that ain't no fair! We can't see your hands!"

Harry replied to the plaintiff loudly, "I was only cold and my friend here was kindly obliging me. But, if you insist, sir," and with those words, he offered his hands to Richard who promptly removed the coat. Harry raised his hands once more, this time no longer chained. He turned and handed the handcuffs to the police Captain and, with a confident, teasing tone said, "Sir, I believe these are yours?"

The startled captain accepted the handcuffs with a bewildered smile as he remarked, "That humble pie went down so fast, I hardly had time to taste it." The crowd erupted into laughter and applause.

As Richard led Harry and Bess along Bridge Street, a throng of excited children ran ahead of them, announcing to everyone within earshot that the Great Houdini had arrived. Several porters trailed behind them with their luggage, and were, in turn, followed by a small group of curious spectators, mostly children.

After a short walk, they arrived at the Phoenix Hotel. Located on the southeast corner of Bridge and Main Street, the hotel was a majestic four-story building, unexpectedly luxurious for such a small town. It had to be, as it often catered to wealthy executives from around the country who were in town to do business with the Phoenix Iron Company.

An eager bellhop awaited them on the front porch and cheerfully showed the party to their room on the second floor. The porters from the train station followed up the stairs carrying the couple's personal luggage. The bellboy opened a door and bid Harry and Bess to enter.

The suite was large, with high ceilings and two rooms. One was a sitting room and the other was a bedroom with a beautiful, ornate brass bed. The porters stacked the luggage by the door and Harry tipped each a quarter in turn as they exited. He tipped the bellboy, as well, before ushering him out and closing the door. Harry turned to Bess, "At last, we have a quiet moment to ourselves."

The couple's solitude was not long lived. A short while later, Richard knocked on their door. The trio rang room service to order a light lunch, which was delivered by the bellhop. While they were eating, Harry inquired about the day's itinerary. Richard wiped his mouth with a white cloth napkin before answering, "The Woolworth's store is just across the street. I had some ironworkers from the factory install a girder system on their roof." Richard pointed out the window, indicating the roof of the building next door. "Everything is set to go, but that won't be until four o'clock. Woolworth's is also loaning us the safe that is on public display in front of the theater, in order to drum up interest in the show and sell tickets."

Harry nodded his head in approval, "Excellent. So, what do we do until four?"

"I scheduled you to appear at an electric park, just a few miles west of town, where there is a Winter Festival today. It's an excellent opportunity to promote tonight's show."

"Speaking of which, what's our competition look like for tonight?" Harry asked as he refilled his cup.

"Phoenixville has three downtown theatres, and they are all very close to each other," Richard answered. "I've booked you in the best of them, the Colonial, a dream palace that is located smack in the middle of town. Meanwhile, Charlie Chaplin's *Pawnshop* is showing at a place called the New-Phoenix, over at Main and Hall Streets, and *Shoes* is showing at the Savoy Theater, just down the street over there," he motioned down Main Street nonchalantly with his finger.

Harry sipped his tea contentedly and placed the china cup back onto its matching saucer as he said with confidence, "Moving pictures, you say? No competition at all! Anyone could see any of those shows on any old night, in any old town. We'll pack the house from miles around."

"Of that, I have no doubt!" Richard exclaimed, rising to his feet and heading for the door. "In fact, it's time I take my leave of you fine people in order to see how things are progressing over at the theater. I'll meet you there. It's on the way to the trolley which runs every hour, so no dilly-dallying, you two!" He shut the door behind him.

The afternoon was brisk, but sunny, as Harry and Bess walked down the steps of the Phoenix Hotel and turned left along Bridge Street. A boy on the corner was selling copies of the Phoenixville Daily Herald, and Harry asked him the way to the trolley stop. The boy pointed down Bridge Street, saying, "You go about two blocks that way, mister. Can't miss it."

Harry reached into his pocket and gave the boy a silver mercury head dime. "Thanks, kid."

A few steps later, the couple paused at the corner while a small, two-seated automobile turned onto Main Street right in front of them. Bess looked at it longingly as it merrily chugged its way up the hill. "Harry, darling, when are we going to get us a Detroiter like that?"

"That, my insatiable little cherub, was a Saxon Roadster. While made in Detroit, it is not a Detroiter," Harry corrected his wife.

"Sounds like a Detroiter to me, smart guy," she teased back.

Harry led her across the hard-packed dirt street. "I was hoping those horseless carriages would just be a passing fad, but I have seen more and more of them just in the last year"

"You may call yourself an escape artist," Bess reproached, "but you are doing a terrible job escaping my question. When are you going to get us one?"

Harry gave her hand a gentle squeeze, "Sweetheart, why would you ever trade a luxurious train ride for one of those contraptions? Besides, how would we transport our trunks? All our stage gear? Our props?"

"Yes, I know, darling. It just looks like fun, is all," Bess answered, obviously avoiding his gaze by looking in the windows of the F.W. Woolworth & Co. store. From across the street, the delicious aroma of freshly baked bread wafted over from a bakery. A block or so behind the bakery and the row of other stores, black smoke billowed up from the coal-fed furnaces at the Iron Works accompanied by the distant ring of hammers banging on iron. As a horse-drawn carriage clattered by, Bess saw their stage manager waving to them. "There's Richard!" she exclaimed, adding excitedly, "and that must be the theater behind him!"

They crossed Bridge Street to meet him. Richard stood under a large sign that hung out over the sidewalk. It read "COLONIAL," in large yellow letters and was lined with electric lights. Over the sidewalk, a marquis advertised that night's show. It read "One Night Only, The Great Houdini." Behind Richard there was a ticket window and the doors to the theater. Standing ominously next to him was a large black Herring Hall Marvin two-door safe. It was just over five feet tall and sitting on four heavy-duty caster wheels, the heavy iron cabinet weighed over 2 tons.

Richard took off his black felt bowler as the couple crossed the street and commented, "I trust you found me without incident. Would you care to inspect the safe, Maestro?"

"Thank you, Richard, but no." Harry acted as though the safe weren't even there. "I trust you have everything arranged inside?"

"Of course. I saw to it personally just a short time ago. I thought certainly you'd want some time to study the safe, however. After all, Harry, this isn't just one of your stage props we're talking about."

"Nonsense. I've yet to meet a lock I couldn't pick and when you think about it, a safe is just a big iron box with a lock on it, isn't it? Doesn't sound too hard." He patted the side of the safe like it was a pet dog.

Bess dropped Harry's other hand and gave Richard an exasperated look. "I tried telling him earlier, but he wouldn't listen to me. Harry, I love you, but sometimes I think you overestimate yourself."

"You both lack faith in me. I'm hurt." He feigned. "Let's go; we wouldn't want to miss the trolley." With that, Harry spun on his heels and started walking away. Bess looked at Richard and rolled her eyes. Richard could only shrug his shoulders in reply as he put his hat back on his head. He motioned down the sidewalk with his open hand, "After you, m'lady."

As the trio walked west down Bridge Street, they passed Angle-moyer's Cash Grocery followed by a tailor, jeweler, haberdashery, hardware store, and an assortment of dry goods stores. One storefront read "Phoenixville Candy Company." Bess pulled on Harry's hand, "Let's get a fountain soda!"

Suddenly, they were interrupted by a clanging bell that announced the approach of the trolley on the set of parallel tracks that ran directly down the middle of the street. Ahead, a small group of people who waited on the hard-packed dirt sidewalk began to move en masse towards the street. The old green trolley had yellow trim and red window sashes. Along the top edge were painted the words "Montgomery & Chester Electric RY."

As the trolley came to a halt, a few people disembarked having arrived at their destination. A tall man wearing a black vest and conductor's hat followed them and then stood by the rail car door. The small crowd of people lined up to pay their fares before boarding the twenty-six-foot-long passenger car. The fare from Phoenixville all the way to Spring City, at the opposite end of the line, was forty cents a head, while the fare to the Bonnie Brae Trolley Park was only twenty cents, located as it was, approximately halfway between the two.

Harry and Bess stepped up to the conductor. "Two for the trolley park, my good man," Harry said as he handed the tall man with the handlebar mustache two silver quarters, each stamped with Lady Liberty on one side and a flying eagle on the reverse. The conductor nodded, giving him a dime in return. As he pocketed the coin, Harry offered Bess his hand, assisting her as she stepped up onto the running board of the car. He grasped the brass handrail and followed, pulling himself aboard.

Despite the cold weather, the car was full of people heading to Bonnie Brae Park to join in the Winter Fest. It only took a moment before one of them recognized Harry and Bess and only a moment more before everyone aboard knew there were celebrities in their midst.

As much as Bess desired to enjoy a quiet ride through the country-side with her husband, she understood that Harry's fame, mixed with his strange brand of magical charisma, drew the other passengers to him and compelled them to engage him in conversation. And Harry, being the consummate showman, would not... no, could not... refuse.

Room was made for them on the bench seat, but Harry grasped the handrail and remained standing as the trolley started rolling. A child seated nearby asked, "Mr. Houdini, sir? Are you a real, true magician?"

Harry looked down at the boy, "Young man, calling Houdini a magician is like calling DaVinci a house painter! Most stage magicians have to purchase their tricks, and almost anyone can be taught to do them. Why, even you! Whereas, I, on the contrary, perform wondrous miracles that boggle the mind!"

"Hey, Houdini! Tell us, what was your closest call?" a man yelled from across the car.

"I am regularly bound-up and thrown into ice-cold rivers, locked in milk cans full of water, any number of feats that could kill me at any time, so, let me assure you, death and I are closely acquainted. The closest I've come to shedding this mortal coil was when I was challenged to escape from the belly of a rotting sea monster that washed up from the deep into Boston Harbor." Cries of astonishment and even some laughter erupted in the car, but Harry simply waited patiently for it to pass before continuing. "I was shackled hand and foot before being forced inside the stinking carcass, which was then wrapped in chains. As you can see, I escaped, but I was nearly suffocated by the fumes from the arsenic they had used to embalm the beast!" The captive audience seemed suitably impressed. For a moment, all one could hear was the clickity-clack of the trolley's wheels riding the rails.

Harry broke the silence, "Enough about me! Isn't Phoenixville the home of the Union Club?"

The riders gave each other looks of surprise. "Damned skippy!" someone called out. "Union Club has been the best football team in Pennsylvania since 1907!" Many aboard cheered their support.

Harry nodded and shouted back, "I can attest to that, sir! A short while back, I saw them eat the Canton Bulldogs alive during a game in Ohio."

Bess smiled as she looked lovingly up at Harry. True, her husband was a skilled magician, but even greater was his skill at showmanship and promotion. In a matter of minutes, he managed to earn the adoration of the entire car of trolley passengers. He knew what his audience wanted, and he gave it to them, and more.

The little trolley began to climb a steep hill and as the steeple of the Zion Lutheran Church came into view, an excited little girl with red curls pulled on her mother's coat and exclaimed, "Mama, we're almost there!"

People began pouring out of the trolley before it fully stopped at the carriage road that ran between the church and the park. The park's entrance was decked with dazzling electric lights that shone brightly even in the middle of the day. As they walked along with the crowd, a man said to Harry and Bess, "Welcome to Bonnie Brae picnic grounds. It means 'beautiful hillside' in Scots."

"It certainly seems to fit the bill," Bess noted happily, "even in winter."

The man went on proudly, "Being next to the church, as it is, Bonnie Brae's an upstanding, family-style picnic park. No gimmicks like charlatans running questionable games here, no sir. Of course, it also means they don't have a dance platform," he added with a tone of regret.

Once inside, Richard turned to Harry and Bess, "You two check things out and meet me at the stage when you are done. I'll go let them know we are here and see to the final arrangements. Don't get lost!"

Harry and Bess took a stroll through the park and took it all in. All around them, the Winter Fest was in full swing. Adults talked and partook of light refreshments, such as hot cider, while children laughed and ran and played. The centerpiece of the park was a resplendent steam-driven carousel, complete with beautiful, brightly painted hand-carved circus animals. Music played cheerily from the calliope as it turned. Other amusements included games, swings, bowling, shuffleboard, and a shooting gallery. Ponies and goats carried children around a fenced circle at the price of a dime a head. At the rear of the park was a small zoo that housed a wide array of animals. There were separate enclosures that housed a surprising array of well-kept animals including a pair of white-tailed deer, a fat old black bear, an ostrich, an Arabian camel, several monkeys, and a bull elk with an immense rack of antlers.

When they completed their quick tour, Harry turned to Bess, took her arm, and remarked, "Very charming, indeed. However, I believe we have a show to put on. Shall we?"

With that, they made their way to a low, open-air platform where a crowd was gathering. On the stage, Richard was speaking to four men holding ropes and chains. When he saw Harry and Bess, he turned to the crowd and spoke loudly, "Ladies and Gentlemen, here he is now, the Great Houdini!"

Harry removed his coat and took seat in the high-backed wooden chair in the center of the stage. The four men began to wrap their ropes and chains around Harry, tying him tightly to the chair. Ten minutes later, they stepped down, their work finally done. Seated in the center of the stage, practically all that could be seen of the Great Houdini was his hands, feet, and head. His torso was completely wrapped in ropes and chains. His legs and arms had been securely tied to the legs and arms of the chair.

The Great Houdini sat nearly motionless, as though he could hardly move a muscle. The minutes ticked by as the crowd watched on with bated breath. Although he remained calm and emotionless, Harry's face grew red with effort and concentration.

Slowly, agonizingly slowly, the Great Houdini's arms began to move beneath his restraints. Then, to the great amazement of the crowd, his shoulders started to shrug, and soon the first loops of rope began to come loose. Twenty minutes later, the Great Houdini was free. He took his bows to great applause as flyers for the evening's performance were passed out to the crowd.

A short time later, Harry, Bess, and Richard caught the trolley back into town. There was still one more stunt to perform before the show.

The streets were packed for as far as the eye could see with people assembled for the afternoon's free entertainment. The Great Harry Houdini would be performing the Hanging Straitjacket Escape for all who came to see.

On the corner of Bridge and Main, Harry stood on a small make-shift stage. With him was a doctor from the Eastern Pennsylvania State Institution for the Feeble-Minded and Epileptic, located in Spring City and later known as Pennhurst State Hospital. The doctor carried with him a white canvas jacket with very long sleeves. Houdini placed his arms into the sleeves, and the crowd cheered wildly as the doctor began to secure its many buckles and belts.

First, the doctor cinched and tightened the back of the straitjacket making sure it was tight around Houdini's chest. Next, a crotch strap went between the performer's legs and was also buckled in the back. Finally, Houdini's arms were crossed in front of his chest and the doctor buckled those straps. "Make sure they're tight there, doc!" a man in front of the stage yelled, before adding, "Don't make it easy for him!"

After completing his task, the doctor stepped back, and representatives from the Phoenixville Hook and Ladder Company stepped up. One looked up and waved. Four stories above the street, another fireman lowered a large hook on the end of a thick hemp rope to the firemen waiting below. The rope ran over a block and tackle hanging from the end of an iron girder that was hanging well out over the sidewalk.

The firemen on stage lowered Harry gently to his back. Harry's ankles were already securely tied with a short, thick length of rope running between his feet and that was looped over the hook on the end of the rope. The firemen on stage waved to their comrade above, who in turn looked behind him and gave a signal to his team on the roof. The rope went taut, and the Great Houdini was slowly hoisted into the air.

Dangling upside down, high over the crowd gave Harry a most stupendous view, and he enjoyed a well-earned rush of adrenaline. He turned his head to look both ways along Bridge Street. It seemed as though the entire town must have turned out for the opportunity to watch the world's greatest escape artist in action. Harry couldn't have asked for more. This escape was not just about promoting his show, it was his gift to all those people who were unable to afford a ticket to one of his shows. It was time to get to work.

As the jacket was sliding onto his arms, Harry inconspicuously pinched some of the material in his hands, and as the doctor was buckling the back of the straitjacket, Harry had taken a huge breath, expanding his chest to its maximum dimensions. When the sleeves were fastened behind him, Harry made sure that his arms were crossed, not folded across his chest, with his stronger right arm on top. He was also careful to exert a constant outward pressure with his arms.

Once in the air, Harry relaxed his muscles and released the material he was holding. The jacket slacked enough to give him the wiggle room he needed. Houdini used his strong arm to force his weaker elbow violently to the left and away from his body. This created more slack around his right shoulder, allowing Harry to pull the right arm over his head. Being upside down enabled him to use gravity to complete this maneuver. Despite popular belief, dislocating his shoulder was not usually a necessary part of the act; however, if all else failed, Harry could do it as a last resort.

Below, the crowd watched with rapt attention as the hanging man wriggled and struggled like a worm dangling from the end of a hook. Houdini's arms were now freed to such an extent that he could reach the straps and buckles of the cuffs with his teeth.

Harry could have performed this escape in much less time than it was actually taking him, but Harry was the consummate showman. He knew that it was important to make the spectacle last long enough to sow doubt in the minds of the crowd as to whether or not the act could even be completed. If he escaped too quickly, the audience would be left with the impression that it was a simple feat that anyone could accomplish.

Once he was free of the cuffs, Houdini was then able to unbuckle his collar and the bottom buckles that secured the strap between his legs. Houdini slipped his arms free when these were undone, and to the great disbelief of the audience, wiggled out of the jacket. The crowd below him erupted in thunderous applause.

The Colonial was a type of new theater known as a "dream palace" due to its fantastically luxurious interior. Many other theaters like it were springing up all across the country. They were designed to cater to a new kind of audience, one that had more demanding standards than the older, working-class one it was replacing. Tonight, the house was packed to capacity, and all three hundred seats were filled.

So far, the evening had been a great success. The act began with a seven-minute film of Houdini in Paris leaping into the Seine handcuffed and escaping, while the house orchestra played a very dramatic piece. After showing this escape, both film and music ended. Harry then walked to center stage and, without saying a word, gazed intensely at his audience until the drop of a pin could have been heard in the large room. In a voice both quiet yet commanding, he then said, "Ladies and Gentlemen, the Crystal Casket."

Two assistants wheeled an empty glass box with transparent sides onto the stage. Houdini walked slowly around the box several times before covering it with a large blue velvet cloth that he seemed to produce suddenly from thin air. Almost as soon as he the box was covered, he whisked the shroud away. There, in the glass box, a girl now appeared. The audience clapped and cheered with surprise. Harry then opened the box and offered Bess a hand as she stepped out. At a time when most women wore dresses down to the ankles, her revealing outfit was nothing short of shocking and a huge hit.

The pair performed many magic tricks and sleights of hand. Houdini made objects appear out of thin air and even float around as though manipulated by ghostly hands. He demonstrated how he became known as the Handcuff King when Captain Gill came out and handcuffed Harry on stage. Within a minute or so, the Great Houdini freed himself, to the amazement of all.

In the act *Good-Bye Winter*, Harry had Bess climb into a box which, as soon as the lid was closed, collapsed in upon itself, revealing that she had mysteriously disappeared. In response, some of the more disappointed men in the audience hissed and booed, egged on by Richard who was planted in the audience. Next, Harry had the Crystal Casket brought out again and made her reappear. With the audience knowing what to expect, the trick went over even better and drew even greater applause.

Next, Harry performed the *East Indian Needle Trick*. Bess presented Harry with a red satin pillow, upon which were fifty silver sewing needles and a coiled length of white silk thread. Houdini called a member of the audience on stage to examine the needles and to verify that they were real. Houdini then placed the needles and thread onto his tongue for all to see and then appeared to swallow all of them by drinking an entire glass of water. Members of the audience were invited on stage to examine his mouth, only to find that it was empty. Houdini then dramatically regurgitated the needles, only now they were threaded together dangling on the string!

In actuality, when Harry pretended to swallow the needles with a drink of water, he really spat the needles and thread into the water glass. He was careful to leave enough water in the glass so that the reflection obscured them. All the while, Houdini kept a packet of needles, already threaded with knots spaced to give the needles a natural play on the thread, concealed between his cheek and gum. It was this thread that Houdini spooled out from his mouth.

Finally, it was time for the grand finale. Houdini was alone on-stage, illuminated by a single spotlight. "Ladies and Gentlemen, you have been a most gracious audience this evening. Normally, I would end my performance with my famous act, *The Chinese Water Torture Cell*, an act in which I am lowered head-first into a tank of water from which to escape, with an assistant always standing by holding an axe at the ready to break the glass in case of an emergency. However, I have been doing that escape for years now, and it is time for a change. As I am sure all of you know, I have been challenged to escape from a burglar-proof safe, provided by your own F.W. Woolworth's Five and Dime, located just across the street."

With that said, a team of four muscular stagehands rolled the heavy safe to center stage. The floorboards creaked under its immense weight. "My lovely assistant and wonderful wife, Bess, can attest to the fact that I have not given this safe so much as a cursory examination before this moment," Houdini continued, "and my stage manager has calculated that the air supply in this particular safe could run out in as little as two minutes. Unlike the *Chinese Water Torture Cell*, there is no way for my assistants to help me should things go wrong."

"A safe like this is impossible to open randomly. The lock is a set of wheels with notches in them. You have to line up the notches on the wheels with contact points. When all the notches are lined up, the lock opens. Since the numbers on the dial go up to 99, anyone would have a one in 99 chance of guessing the first number of the combination. The probability of randomly selecting the correct second number shoots up to one in 9,702. However, the odds of randomly finding the correct position for *all* three wheels is one in 941,094, not quite one in a million, but not far off. Naturally, I will not be able to reach the combination dial as I will be locked inside the safe. I cannot emphasize how dangerous this feat will be. I will be risking an agonizing death by suffocation in two minutes, should I fail to escape."

Captain Gill came back on stage and searched Harry head to toe. He took Harry's belt and shoes, then declared to the audience, "He's clean," and walked off stage again. With that, Harry crawled inside the safe. Just before Bess closed the heavy iron doors, she shot him a worried look. Harry just smiled and winked.

The doors shut with a heavy thud. Bess turned the handle, spun the dial, and stepped away. Two stagehands emerged from the wings with a velvet screen and placed it in front of the safe. Another stagehand brought out an oversized clock and placed it on an easel for everyone to see. The orchestra began to play as the spellbound audience watched the seconds start ticking away.

Inside the safe, Harry was suddenly enveloped in complete darkness. He could hear the faint, muffled sound of the orchestra playing. Richard sent him the make and model of this safe ahead of time so Harry would know exactly what type he would be dealing with. Not only was Harry an expert on various designs of locks and safes, but he had also spent his entire adult life training his body and mind to a superhuman level.

First, he contracted the muscles in his throat to regurgitate a small, egg-shaped container that he held suspended in his esophagus, a trick he had learned on the vaudeville circuit. Next, he opened the capsule and felt the small tools contained inside to find the one he needed. He then ran his finger along the edge of the safe door to locate the heads of the screws that needed to be removed in order to gain access to the safe's locking mechanism.

After a few moments, he had removed six of the twelve screws that secured the metal panel that was the inside of the door. He carefully pulled the metal sheet away from the frame enough so that he could slip his hand inside and feel the locking wheels. Next, Houdini used his phenomenal finger sensitivity to detect the very slight imbalance created by the notches in the wheels as he turned them. He adjusted the notch on the first wheel, then the second. Finally, when the notch on the third wheel was directly under the fence, he felt the bar fall into place. Now, he could move the activating lever and unlock the handle.

Meanwhile, outside the safe, the clock on stage continued to tick the seconds away. The audience began to grow restless. More time passed, and the audience grew concerned. Long past the two-minute mark, they began to panic.

Audience members, again encouraged by Richard hiding in the crowd, started demanding that the stage managers open the safe. When it appeared that the audience could take no more and at exactly the right moment, the Great Houdini emerged from behind the screen, upon which Bess ran out from the wings, jumped into his arms, and kissed him. The audience, sharing her relief, broke out into laughter and applause.

Always a Showman.

Epilogue

Harry Houdini was a master of promotion. He kept his name in the papers by performing new and unusual, often dangerous and even deadly, stunts, the likes of which no one had ever seen. The press was his tool of choice, and he used every opportunity deftly to promote his own exploits to the benefit of himself and those around him. His sense of showmanship allowed him to make even basic escapes seem like the most dangerous and impressive feats in the world.

We don't know for sure that Houdini performed his *Hanging Strait-jacket Escape* during his brief visit to Phoenixville; however, we do know that he frequently performed this act a few hours before his evening shows. We do know that he escaped from a burglar-proof safe. Whatever else he may have included in his performance that day, I'm sure that everyone who had the privilege of seeing Houdini in Phoenixville that day would have to agree that the undisputed King of Vaudeville put on a memorable show.

~ Chapter Nine ~
Hollywood on the Pickering:
The Tale of The Blob

September 26th, 1950:

Veteran Philadelphia police officers Joe Keenan and John Collins saw what appeared at first to be a parachute drifting down from the sky. Upon investigation, they discovered a mass of purple jelly laying on the ground, approximately six feet in diameter and a foot thick in the middle. The pulsating mass was filled with glittering crystals and gave off a strange mist. When the officers turned off their flashlights, the jelly produced a soft glow.

Keenan and Collins called for backup, and two more officers soon arrived. Sergeant Joe Cook scooped up a handful of the material, and it instantly broke into small globules that evaporated in his hand, leaving a sticky, odorless residue on his skin.

The local FBI was notified, but agents didn't arrive in time to witness anything. Within thirty minutes, the mass evaporated entirely. The officers reported that whatever it was had been so light that it had not even bent the grass beneath it. All four witnessing officers believed that the "star jelly" had been some sort of living organism.

Jack Harris was sitting by the fire in the living room of his Philadelphia home sharing a drink with his friend, Irvine Millgate, professor of humanities at Northwestern University. The professor leaned forward and advanced a pawn on the chessboard that sat on the low table between them. "Enough about me, Jack. How did you get into the movie business?"

"Between you and me, I cut my teeth in vaudeville singing and dancing with Ukulele Ike's Kiddie Revue, when I was just six. And let it never be spoken of again!" Jack emptied what was left in his glass in a single gulp. "I got a job as a theater usher straight out of high school, and within five years I was managing sixteen movie houses. When the war came, I did a stint with Army intelligence overseas, and when I came home, I went into publicity. A few years later, I made the jump to film distribution. I now have offices in Philadelphia, Pittsburgh, and Washington." He moved his bishop to take one of the professor's pawns.

"Congratulations, Jack. Sounds like you are doing well for yourself." The professor took the bishop with his knight.

"Good enough that I'm ready to move up the ladder. I want to produce my own films. You ought to see the quality of some of the B-movies that I have to deal with. Yet, they make money. I'm sure I can do better."

"Are you planning on moving to Hollywood, Jack?"

"No, I don't think that will be necessary. I know an independent production company located just on the other side of Valley Forge. I'm thinking of doing something exciting, like a monster movie! All I need is an idea." Jack moved his rook to the king's row. "Checkmate."

"Well played, Jack." The professor sat back and sipped his drink as he thought for a moment. "It seems that science fiction is becoming very popular. How about an alien race that comes to Earth to hunt, but just for sport, like trophy hunters on safari, only these aliens hunt humans! Imagine how formidable an intergalactic safari hunter would be, equipped with all kinds of advanced weaponry and technology."

"No, that wouldn't work. Aliens played by men in cheap costumes are all played out. They're a dime a dozen! I need a movie monster that isn't some guy dressed up in a suit. I need something new, something that has never been done before."

The two sat in silence for a while, enjoying their drinks and staring into the fire. The Professor finally spoke, "Do you remember an article in the *Philadelphia Inquirer* a few years back, about two Philly cops who found some kind of space jelly?"

"Space jelly? No, I must have missed that one," Jack pondered. "Tell me about it."

"It was like a big glob of purple goo. The cops who saw it said it was pulsating as though it were alive."

"Hmmm... sounds strange, but it doesn't sound very scary."

"One of the officers decided it would be a good idea to stick his hand in the stuff. Darwinism at work," the professor chuckled.

"What happened?" Jack asked.

"Nothing. The stuff just kind of evaporated. Lucky for him, let me tell you. Just imagine if that stuff were alive! Or, if it was some kind of parasite?"

Jack put his drink down next to the chessboard and leaned closer. "Parasite? You mean, like a tick?"

"Actually, I was thinking of something more like a giant amoeba, an amorphous mass that would dissolve and absorb whatever organic matter it came in contact with."

Jack was excited now. "And every time it ate something, it could get... bigger and bigger!"

The professor smiled back. "Yes, I suppose it could."

Jack sprang out of his seat and started pacing the room. "And the method of killing the monster would have to be something that grandma could have cooked up on her stove."

The professor sat back and swilled his drink. "How about grandma's freezer? Most amoebae are killed or go dormant in cold temperatures."

The phone rang several times before it was answered by a tall man with rolled-up sleeves. "Valley Forge Film Studios. How may I help you?"

"Hello, this is Jack Harris. I was hoping to speak with Reverend Yeaworth."

"Hello, Jack! It's me! How are things in the big city?"

"Can't complain, Shorty. How are things at Good News Productions?"

"Wonderful, Jack. Thank you. Since we made the move to Yellow Springs, I couldn't be happier. What can I do for you?"

"Excuse me if I just cut to the chase, Reverend. I know you specialize in religious films, but I want you to make me a different kind of movie... a monster movie! But, not like those run-of-the-mill cheapy-creepies. It's gotta be in color instead of black and white. Do you think you could handle it?"

"Jack, I own a whole village a few miles south of Phoenixville. I have production managers, directors, scriptwriters, sound recorders, photographers, cameramen, prop men, lighting technicians, and of course, actors. Why, I even have my own press representatives!"

"That sounds great! How about special effects? I've got an idea for a unique monster, something that's never been done before."

"I've got a few talented animators. What do you have in mind, Jack?"

"It's called 'The Molten Meteor.' It's a sci-fi, horror movie about a meteorite that falls to Earth near a small town. Inside the space rock is a mysterious creature from another planet. It looks like nothing you've ever seen before, a mass of jelly that eats every human it encounters. And, get this, every time the creature eats someone, it grows larger and more powerful. By the end of the movie, it has grown into a gigantic, seemingly unstoppable monster!"

"Sounds interesting. You might have something here, Jack. Do you have a script?"

"Not yet. I was hoping you could help me with that, too. I want it to have some substance. It's gotta have characters that you can believe in. I was thinking some teenagers find the monster first, but since no one will believe their story, it's up to the kids. Until they can stop it and save everyone, the creature just keeps on getting bigger and more deadly."

"I think we can work with that, just give me a few days to get some storyboards together. Then, if you can come visit for a few days, we can work through the details."

"Thanks, Reverend... or should I say, '*Director*'?"

A few days later, Jack Harris and Reverend Irvin "Shorty" Yeaworth stood in the middle of the quiet country road that ran in front of the Yellow Springs Inn and Tavern. It was a beautiful day in late May, a bright, sunny afternoon tempered by a gentle breeze that rustled through the leaves of the trees high overhead. "Wow, Reverend, this place is beautiful!"

"Thanks, Jack. Before I bought it a few years ago, this place was the Country School for the Pennsylvania Academy of the Fine Arts. I like to think of it as my own little slice of heaven, the perfect place to do the Good Lord's work. And please, call me 'Shorty.' Everyone else does."

Jack looked confused. "You're a pretty tall guy to be nick-named Shorty. If you don't mind my asking, how did you get that nick-name?"

"It's not a very interesting story, I'm afraid. You see, my name is Irvin S. Yeaworth Junior. The 'S' stands for Shortess. It's a family name."

"Shortess, huh? That must have made growing up extra fun." Jack gazed down the picturesque slope at some buildings that could just be seen peeping out of the thick foliage under a grove of large elms. "Are those spring houses?"

"Yes. There are actually three natural springs here. Each one carries a different mineral from deep inside the earth. There's an iron spring, a magnesium spring, and a sulfur spring. The Indians used this place until 1722 when it became a health spa. During the Revolutionary War, George Washington commissioned the con-struction of that building there to house sick soldiers from Valley Forge." Shorty motioned to the fieldstone building on the hill behind the Inn and continued, "It was the first military hospital in America. Now, it is Studio B, the editing facility for Good News Productions."

The Village at Yellow Springs
1) Inn at Yellow Springs, 2) Main House, 3) Lincoln Building,
4) Hospital/Studio B, 5) Studio A, 6) Jenny Lind House, 7) Studio C.

"So, you own the whole town?" Jack asked, in amazement.

"Well, it's more of a village than a town, but yes, I do, all one hundred forty-two acres plus eleven buildings." He pointed down Art School Road. "Everything down to the barn over there, which we call Studio C. We converted the two old hotels to apartments, so we have plenty of room for everyone to live on site. We're one big happy family of filmmakers. I like to call this place, 'Hollywood on the Pickering.'" Shorty gave Jack a wink and a smile. "We're heading to that barn across the street. That's where the story-boards are set up."

Inside the main room of Studio A, a series of sketches were pre-sented on a dozen or so easels set up in a semi-circle. A man and a woman were quietly inspecting them. They turned when they heard Shorty's voice.

"Jack, it is my pleasure to introduce you to Theodore Simonson and Kate Phillips." The two waved. "Theodore is a minister, and Kate is actually former actress Kay Linaker. She was in *Kitty Foyle* with Ginger Rogers. They are Good News Production's most talented writers. I've called upon them to write our screenplay."

Shorty gave Jack a moment to exchange pleasantries with Kate and Theodore before he went on, "Jack and I have worked out the major sequences. Of course, it will be up to you two to fill in the gaps. Jack, as the producer of this film, I give you the honors."

"Thanks, Reverend... I mean, Shorty." They looked at the first sketch of the opening title. In spooky, oozing letters it read, "*The Glob*." Jack turned to Theodore and Kate. "We were originally going to call it *The Molten Meteorite*, but Shorty here feels like *The Glob* is more ominous."

Theodore spoke up, "Yes, sir. About that, please excuse me, sir... but Kate and I were just discussing the title when you came in. You see, I believe *The Glob* is already a book, one by Walt Kelly. It's a children's book about the evolution of man." He shook his head in stern disapproval. "Very un-Christian."

Jack and Shorty exchanged glances, shrugged, and then Jack gave in, saying, "Okay. So, maybe we'll have to change the title. Let's move on." Jack motioned to the first group of pictures, sketched on large sheets of paper in colored pastels. "In our opening shot, two teenagers, Steve Andrews and his girl, Jane, are parked in a convertible on a country road under the stars. They see a very close shooting star and decide to try to find where it landed."

They moved on to the next series of illustrations. "Meanwhile, an old man who lives alone in the country sees the meteor impact close to his shack and goes to investigate. He finds a strange jelly-like substance that gets onto his hand, and he can't get it off. Steve and Jane find him and take him to the town doctor. Soon the man is totally absorbed. Unfortunately, the doctor and his nurse become the glob's next victims."

Again, a new series of sketches. "Steve goes to the police, but by the time they get back to the doctor's, the glob has moved off in search of more prey. Finding little evidence, the cops don't know what to think. Meanwhile, the creature finds an unwary garage mechanic that is working late and eats him up, before moving on to the town grocery store, owned by Steve's father, for a midnight snack." The group moved on to the next series of sketches.

"On their way home, Steve and Jane notice that the store is open but deserted, so they decide to check it out. The glob tries to eat them, but they hide in the store's walk-in freezer. The monster starts to ooze in under the door, but then retreats, foreshadowing the creature's only weakness."

"Knowing that the cops won't believe them, Steve rounds up a bunch of his teenage friends, and they make enough of a racket to gather a crowd downtown. As Steve is trying to warn them, the entire audience of the theater across the street bursts through its door, fleeing and screaming into the streets. The police chief realizes... finally... that something is seriously wrong."

"By now, the monster is huge. Steve and Jane hide out in a diner, but the creature traps them inside. The police try to kill the monster by dropping a power line on it, but all that does is set the diner on fire. As Steve is putting out flames with a CO^2 extinguisher, he sees the creature recoil. Remembering how it retreated from the freezer earlier, Steve figures out that the creature's weakness is the cold and yells this to his friends outside."

"Here, in this final series of pictures, we see the other kids breaking into the high school to retrieve more extinguishers, which they use to attack and freeze the monster. The creature is then airlifted to the Arctic by the Air Force, where it will hopefully remain frozen forever. The end. What do you think?"

Kate took a deep breath and responded, "Well, it is certainly different from anything else we've done."

Theodore said, "I like the idea of a monster with no form. There's something quite refreshing about an unearthly threat with neither a goofy face nor some complicated higher purpose. It simply wants to consume. It's so *alien*. I love it!"

Jack added, "I see this as a teenage movie, modeled on films like James Dean's *Rebel Without a Cause* and *Blackboard Jungle*, only I want to sympathize with today's youth by showing their good side."

Kate and Theodore nodded their heads in approval. "We can get behind that," Ted agreed.

Shorty smiled. "Great! You two get to work. Meanwhile, we'll begin casting the main characters."

Jack Harris walked into the nineteenth-century barn that stood at the end of the village, Studio C. He had pep in his step and a smile on his face. He approached a group of men who were working on the set of a small cabin in the woods. The shack was practically the size of a doll's house, not more than three feet high. "Hey, fellas, that looks great! But why is the cabin so small? I mean, I'm going to need to find some pretty small actors to shoot on *that* set!"

Shorty Yeaworth looked up and smiled at Jack. He told the men to keep working, then turned and walked over to greet him. "This is for the scene where the old man finds the meteor. We use it in the background of wide shots to create a false perspective. It makes the small cabin look far away in the shot."

Jack dismissed Shorty's explanation with a wave. "Yes, I know. I was just joking. Hey, Shorty," he continued, "have I got some big news for you!"

"Excellent. So, do I. Good news abounds!"

Jack motioned politely as he said, "You go first. What's new in Studio C?"

Shorty smiled. "Well, as you can see, the sets are going well... and... oh yeah, I received a package this morning from Pittsburg."

Jack couldn't contain his excitement. "You mean, it's here? Really? Where? Can I see it? How's it look? Do you think it's going to work?"

Shorty had to laugh. "Woah there, tiger. Your baby is right over there, in that can." He motioned to a black five-gallon bucket like the ones used for driveway sealant or roofing tar. Jack was like a kid on Christmas morning. He ran over and pried the lid off the can. He tipped the bucket so the dim light inside the studio illuminated its contents. Then, a smile broke on his face, and without hesitation, he reached inside with his hand. Shorty laughed again. "You're as bad as the old man in our movie, Jack, sticking your fingers into things without a second thought."

Jack laughed at the comparison. "I guess you're right. Wow, this stuff is out of this world! It feels really strange. And, not sticky at all." He let some of the ooze drip between his fingers back into the bucket. "Silicone, huh? This stuff is perfect! And they said it would never dry out. Look how clear it is! The guy at Union Carbide said we can color it by mixing in vegetable dye. I figured we could make it increasingly redder as it consumes more victims."

Shorty smiled and pointed at Jack exclaiming, "That's genius! I love how your brain works." He then added, "So, what's your big news?"

Jack put the lid securely back onto the pail, stepped back, and proudly announced, "I found our Steve Andrews!"

"That's excellent, Jack! I think Franciosa will be perfect for the part."

"Well...uh..., I didn't actually sign Anthony Franciosa."

"What?!" Shorty reacted incredulously, "You mean he didn't want the part?"

"I never asked him. You see, I found someone even *better*! I went to see *A Hatful of Rain* like you suggested, and while Franciosa was certainly up to his role, it was an understudy that was filling in for another actor that really stole the show. This kid has charisma. He could be the next James Dean."

"Okay, Jack, okay! You sold me. What's his name?"

"Steven McQueen."

The smile melted immediately from Shorty's face as he asked, "Who?"

"Steven McQueen. At twenty-eight, he's a little old for the part, but I think he can pull off being a teenager. Trust me, Shorty, I know talent when I see it. He's perfect. I can't wait for you to meet him."

Shorty frowned. "Oh, I've met him, all right! His girlfriend is Neile Adams. She appeared in a short religious film we did last year. Steve was always with her, like an annoying shadow that wouldn't shut up. I'm telling you, Jack, that dirty jerk is an opinionated pain in the ass! As soon as she was done her lines, I kicked him off the set. Now, you're telling me that *he's* the star of *our* movie?!"

Jack shrugged. "I'm afraid so, Shorty. I was so excited that I already signed him."

Shorty looked away and huffed. After a moment he looked back at Jack and asked, "What did he agree to?"

"I offered him what we were going to offer Franciosa, $2,500 or 10% of the final take."

"And? Which did he choose?"

"He said a bird in the hand was worth two in the bush, so he took the money."

Shorty gave a short, humorless laugh as he mused out loud, "I know a good Christian shouldn't entertain such thoughts, but imagine how it would feel to be Mr. McQueen if we get really lucky and this flick grosses some seriously big bucks?"

A week later, about fifty cast and crew were assembled in Studio A for a production meeting. Shorty opened the meeting. "Welcome, everyone! As you know, we begin filming 'The Blob' tomorrow, so I thought it would be a good idea if we all got to know each other and finalize the shooting schedule. For those of you who missed the read-through, this film is about an oozing, amoeba-like alien that travels to Earth inside a meteorite, then expands as it sucks up people and menaces a small town in Pennsylvania."

"I think you all know me, but just for formality's sake, I am Shorty Yeaworth, your director. This man is our producer, Jack Harris." Jack smiled and waved to the group. "Jack has already made a name for himself in the film distribution industry. Like so many of us here, this will be his first foray into creating a feature-length film." The small group broke out into a short smattering of spontaneous applause.

Shorty motioned to a young man lounging in a folding chair, his right ankle propped up on his left knee, casually smoking a Marlboro cigarette. "The lead role of Steve Andrews will be played by the aptly named Steve McQueen." Steve acknowledged them all with a scant nod of his head. He wore a hip tan cotton jacket over a beige collared shirt, and his gray strap-in-the-back slacks were also a popular fashion trend. As if to keep the young buck in his place, Shorty added, "This will be Steve's big-screen debut."

"Our heroine will be played by Miss Aneta Corsaut." He motioned to a pretty, auburn-haired girl with dazzling blue eyes, set off by her fuzzy white Angora rabbit-hair sweater accented by a light blue neck scarf, tied to one side, that was just enough to add a splash of color. Her blue felt swing skirt fell just below her knees. She waved shyly to the group as Shorty continued, "We had a hard time finding our perfect Jane. In fact, it was only yesterday that Aneta tried out for the part, but we knew right away that we finally found the right actress for the role." The assembled crowd smiled and offered Aneta gestures of their approval.

"Filming begins tomorrow in and around the village. The old man's cabin and the crater are set up on the soundstage in Studio C for the beginning of the film." Shorty motioned to an older man seated off to one side, slightly away from the largely younger members assembled. "Olin Howland, here, will play the unfortunate farmer who first encounters the creature." The older gentleman stood half-way out of his chair, smiled, and waved briefly before letting gravity pull him back down. Shorty added reverently, "Ole has more film experience than all of us put together. He started doing silent films back in the 20s and worked his way up to become one of the top western stars of the 40s. However, most of you younger folks would probably recognize Ole from his recent appearance on *I Love Lucy*, when he played the owner of a rundown diner and motel." A murmur of recognition and admiration ran through the group.

"Next week, we pack up for our first location shoot, in Phoenixville. First, we'll be at Main Street and 3rd Avenue, at the southwest corner of Reeve's Park. This will be the doctor's office where Steve takes the old guy after finding him with the alien parasite stuck on his hand."

"From there, we do a short scene at the Automotive Garage, located at Route 23 and Mowere Road, where the Blob gobbles up a mechanic that is working late. Since all of the special effects will be added later, it should be a simple shoot."

"The following week, we move to Jerry's Supermarket on the north side of Royersford. For those of you who don't get up there much, it's on the corner of Lewis and Oak. This will be where Steve and Jane hide from the Blob in the freezer. We'll also shoot a few other scenes at the same time. We've arranged to have a fire truck and some men from the nearby Sinclair volunteer fire department to meet us there within just a few hours of notice, so long as they don't get a call, of course."

"In week three, we'll be shooting footage for the movie's climax at the Downingtown Diner, on Lancaster Avenue. This shoot is out of order from the script, of course, but it will give our art director, Bart Sloane... raise your hand, Bart... there he is... it will give Bart and his crew more time to get started on creating the matte paintings he needs for the animated sequences, such as the electric line being shot off of the pole and electrocuting the Blob. If you haven't seen this wizard at work, you should. He uses an animation technique where he projects live-action images onto a glass panel and traces over them to create amazing, cutting-edge special effects. What do you call that again, Bart?"

"It's called rotoscoping," Bart answered with a sense of pride, "but we also use standard animation, stop animation, reverse photography, and a whole host of other optical tricks." The technical jargon impressed the group into silence, although it did raise some eyebrows.

Shorty broke the silence. "Week four should be our final week of shooting, and we'll be back in Phoenixville. The first location will be the Memorial Junior High School on Second Avenue, where the kids go to get the fire extinguishers to freeze the Blob. Our second and final location will be the Colonial Theater, downtown on Bridge Street, where the Blob eats a whole theater full of kids. But that shoot is still several weeks away. We have a lot of film to shoot between now and then. I suggest everyone get a good night's sleep. I'll see you all tomorrow morning at eight AM sharp in Studio C. Don't be late!"

The sun was just going down when Jack turned off Nutt Road onto Second Avenue. The last few weeks went pretty smoothly. They had completed shoots on locations in Phoenixville, Royersford, and Downingtown. Now, they were back in Phoenixville for the final week of filming. As he approached the intersection at Lincoln Avenue, he could see that the road ahead was closed. The lawn in front of Memorial Junior High School was packed with lights, soundmen, and cameras. Jack turned down Lincoln Avenue, parked his car, and then walked back to the school where he found Shorty working out the last-minute details of the scene. "Hey Shorty, how's it going?"

"Hello, Jack. As well as can be expected, I suppose. The actual street, Second Avenue there, was too far from the entrance for a good shot, so as you can see, we decided to use the sidewalk instead. The kids will drive up in the blue convertible, stop here, and run to the front door. Then, we'll reset the cameras and lighting for close-up shots of the window getting broken and the kids rushing in to get the fire extinguishers."

"You're going to break the window? Are you sure the school will be cool with that?"

"I already have a crew member standing by with a replacement pane of glass. We have glazing and everything," Shorty replied confidently, adding, "Before we leave, it will be like it never even happened."

Jack nodded. "Sounds great, Shorty. It looks like you have things well in hand. Do you think you'll finish up here tonight?"

"Yeah, I think we'll be able to get everything we need. Barring any unforeseen complications, I'd say we should be out of here by eleven, at the latest."

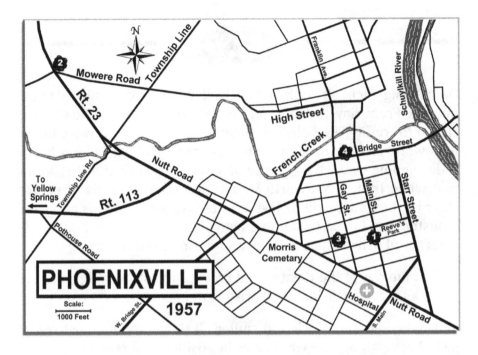

Phoenixville Filming Locations for *The Blob*

1) Dr. Hallen's Office: northwest corner of Main Street at 3rd Avenue
2) Automotive Garage: northwest corner of Rt 23 and Mowere Rd
3) Memorial Junior High School: 320 Second Avenue
4) The Colonial Theater: 227 Bridge Street

"Fantastic. I'm going downtown to let the folks at the Colonial know that we are on schedule to start shooting there tomorrow. Since there are no windows in the theater, we can start the interior shots early and shoot all day. Then, we just have that last scene to shoot on Saturday night. I'll stop by the stationhouse, as well, to make sure they have a few extra officers on standby to close the street off for us."

"Thanks, Jack. By now everyone in town has heard that we're shooting a monster movie. I had the kids put the word out that we are looking for volunteers on Saturday night. I anticipate we'll get a good-sized crowd."

On the big night, it looked like Hollywood had come to Phoenixville. From Gay to Main, an entire block of Bridge Street was closed to traffic. The Colonial Theater sparkled as if it were brand new while crowds of people stood eagerly waiting behind barricades hoping to catch a glimpse of a monster. Little did they know that while Irvin S. Yeaworth Jr. sat impressively in his director's chair by the camera giving last minute instructions to his crew, the monster they hoped to see was actually miles away, resting safely in its metal pail inside a non-descript barn in Yellow Springs.

Jack came out of the theater and crossed the street. "Hey, Shorty, we're all set to go inside. How are you doing out here?"

Shorty looked up at Jack and smiled, "I think we're almost ready, Jack! I have all our camera crews in position and ready to go. One is in the cherry picker over there, and a second is in that open window above the variety store across the street. Three more are on street level, two on tripods and one hand-held. I think we'll get all the footage we need."

"Excellent. Remember, when the first person runs out of the theater, start rolling. Thirty seconds later, I'll release the rest of them."

"Roger that," Shorty replied. "How long do you need?"

"Not long." Jack smiled and asked, "Are you having as much fun as I am?"

"I'm having the time of my life, Jack." Shorty offered Jack his hand and said with a huge smile as Jack shook it, "Good luck."

Jack shook it solemnly. "To both of us," he replied, nodding his head. Then Jack turned and crossed the street back to the theater.

Behind him, Shorty yelled, "Places, everybody! Three minutes to shoot! Clear the set!"

Inside the Colonial, the theater was packed with people who volunteered to be in the movie. People from all walks of life were there. There were young people still in their teens, others who were older, and professional people from throughout the community. It was as though everyone came out for a chance to be in a monster movie.

Jack ran down the aisle and jumped up onto the stage. His unplanned dramatic entrance made a bigger impression than he intended; however, he was pleased when the chatter in the large room immediately quieted down. An air of anticipation washed over the crowd as he began to speak, "Ladies and Gentlemen, I thank you all for coming here tonight. We all know why we're here. Without you, none of this would be possible."

He continued in a deep, suspenseful voice, "A strange, amoeba-like creature from outer space has landed in the countryside just outside of this quiet little town. All evening this amorphous blob has been making its way closer and closer to the center of town, growing bigger and bigger as it consumes everyone and everything it encounters. Now, unbeknownst to you, the audience, the monster has invaded this very theater. It has quietly slithered into the projection booth and, at this very moment, is devouring the technician, dissolving his body, and turning him into more of the Blob."

Jack gave a subtle signal, brushing his hair back with his hand, and a young man waiting in the back slipped quietly out into the lobby. When the door closed behind him, he abruptly ran out of the theater into the deserted street where the young man waved his arms twice before running off to one side. Amplified by his megaphone, Shorty's voice echoed off the buildings, "Roll cameras!"

Inside the theater, Jack continued, "The creature lives to eat. It senses you, the unwitting audience gathered innocently to watch, ironically enough, a midnight spook show." Jack's voice grew in volume as he said, "The Blob squeezes its red, jelly-like body through the holes in the back wall and lunges into the room. Everyone the slime touches is being eaten ALIVE! You see their skin dissolving as they scream painfully in horror. And now, it's trying to eat *you!* Run, everyone! Run for your lives! RUN!!!!"

As the audience leapt out of their seats and ran screaming from the theater, Jack got a sudden inspiration. He leapt off the stage and joined the screaming crowd running for the exit.

"It's hard to believe it's been three months since we finished filming, Jack. Time sure does fly. Do you miss it?"

"Yeah, those were some good times. We'll have to film another one, sometime. I have an idea for a movie called '4D Man'. It's not going to star Mr. Steve McQueen, that's for sure. You were being too kind when you called that kid an opinionated ass. He's certainly become a pain in mine!"

"Hate to say I told you so," Shorty laughed, "but, I told you so! Steve drove me nuts, especially his chain-smoking on set. He kept thinking he could just hide his lit cigarette while doing his lines. What a buffoon! What'd he do that rocked your boat?"

"It's just his attitude, I guess. The last straw was when I asked him to redub some of the dialogue." Jack frowned. "Everything has to be an argument with him, and rest assured, he's always right. I can't believe I signed him for three pictures. That contract is going in the trash. I swear I'm never working with him again. Hey, let's forget about him. Give me some good news. How are the special effects coming along?"

Shorty took a deep breath before responding, "Slowly, I'm afraid. At this rate, it could take another six months to finish. There's just so much to do. Bart and his crew have to construct a bunch of mini-sets to use as backgrounds for almost every shot that the Blob appears in to make it look bigger than it is. They are also working on an animated main title sequence over which the cast and credits can then be matted. Speaking of which, have you heard anything back about the title song, yet? You know, *Blackboard Jungle* used 'Rock Around the Clock', and that song went to number one for eight weeks, driving up box office sales something crazy. Kids who loved the song went to see the movie."

"I think you're really going to like this," Jack said, pepped up at the change of subject. "We have a talented young writer, named Burt Bacharach, working on it. He played a little of it for me over the phone. It was catchy and kitschy. It went something like, 'Beware of the Blob, it creeps, and leaps, and glides, and slides across the floor, right through the door... yada yada, dada da'... anyway, you get the idea. He said they recorded it with a professional session singer, someone named Burt Knee, but apparently it just fell flat. Luckily, Burt started playing around with the track in the studio and ended up overlapping it five times, which gave it a cool, spooky feel. They joked about saying it was by the 'Five Blobs.' I told them to call themselves whatever they wanted and to just send us a tape by the end of next week."

"The end of next week, huh?" Shorty mused. "What's the rush? I told you the special effects team would need a few months."

Jack smiled a sly grin. "Shorty... I have some big news for you."

"Big news, huh?"

"Oh yes." Jack smiled and explained, "I wanted to wait until I was sure, which I'm still not yet, but things are looking really good, so...."

"For crying out loud, Jack," Shorty exclaimed, "will you spill the beans already?!"

"Paramount Pictures wants to buy *The Blob*!"

"They do?!"

"They do. I told them it cost us $240,000."

"But, Jack, that's more than twice our budget!"

"I know. I am such a dastardly rascal."

"So, how much did they say they were willing to pay?"

"I got them up to..." Jack cleared his throat dramatically before saying, "Three hundred thousand dollars!"

Shorty looked amazed. He did some quick figuring in his head and shouted, "Jack, that's almost a 200% profit!"

Jack smiled slyly. "I know," he declared with a wink.

Shorty sat up quickly, a pleased expression growing on his face. "Well, well, Mr. Big-Time Movie Producer," he said after a moment, getting up to prepare two glasses, "I'd say *this* calls for a toast!"

Epilogue

"'Wagner's music,' said Mark Twain, 'is better than it sounds.' You could say something like that about this classic 50s horror movie. It's better than it has any right to be." - Norman N. Holland

Shot over the course of just 31 days during the summer of 1957, and on a budget of only $110,000, *The Blob* was an independent film entirely without Hollywood polish. However, that didn't keep *The Blob* from becoming a sizeable hit for Paramount that billed it as a double feature with *I Married A Monster From Outer Space*. *The Blob* was especially well liked by teenagers and drive-in audiences. Aided by Burt Bacharach's bouncy theme song, the film raked in nearly four million dollars at the box office and helped to launch the independent cinema movement.

The mixture of red dye and silicone that comprised the Blob has never dried out and is still kept in the original five-gallon bucket in which it was shipped from Union Carbide in 1957. The Blob is occasionally put on display as a part of Blobfest, an annual three-day event held each summer in Phoenixville. In addition to the original Blob, you can see other props from the movie, such as miniature sets used in production, and the actual hot rod and fire truck that appeared in the film. During the Blobfest, the-still-functioning Colonial Theater features multiple screenings of *The Blob* and other horror films. There are other fun events also, such as a film competition, a screaming contest, and a street fair that features vendors and live entertainment. The highlight of the festival is a live reenactment of the most famous scene of the film, when the panicked audience rushes out of the theater to escape the BLOB!

~ Chapter Ten ~

The Curse of the Old Mill:
The Rise and Fall of Phoenix Steel

Present Day

It was a picture-perfect summer day in downtown Phoenixville. The morning sun was shining brightly, making every color seem incredibly vibrant. A light breeze rustled through the leaves of a maple tree growing along the sidewalk of Main Street, and the sunlight shining through its leaves created a glittering pattern of light on the sidewalk. A bird chirped and took flight as a door opened, and two figures emerged from Brown's Cow Ice Cream Shop stepping out into crisp morning air.

The smaller of the two stopped, turned, and looked up with consternation on his young face. "Pop-pop, my hands are too full. Can you carry my library books for me while I eat my ice cream?"

The older man looked down at his grandson, a thoughtful look on his face and a twinkle in his eye, and replied, "I imagine I *could*."

The boy rolled his eyes and asked again, "*Will* you hold my books for me, Pop-pop, please? I don't want to drop them, and I sure wouldn't want to get ice cream on them."

"It would be my pleasure," the old man answered, reaching for the books, only to withdraw his hands suddenly with a sly grin as the boy went to hand them to him. "That is... for a taste of that ice cream!" The boy hesitated and then tentatively held the cone up for his grandfather. "Thank you. You know, mint chocolate chip is my sixth favorite flavor of ice cream." The boy smiled as the old man took the books from him. The pair turned left and started slowly down the hill.

As they walked, the boy concentrated on his ice cream, while the older man looked around. "Imagine, a long time ago, all of this used to be woods."

The boy took a brief pause from his ice cream, then, barely turning his head, asked, "How long ago?"

"Three hundred years. Back then, the only people who lived here were Indians. The hills were covered with trees, the streams were full of fish, and the forest was full of animals like deer, turkeys, bears, and even wolves. A frontiersman named Moses Coates came here and built a log hut on the other side of French Creek. Do you remember what the Indians called it?"

The boy thought for a bit as he licked melted ice cream from his fingers. "The *Native Americans* called it the Sankanac." The two stopped at the corner of Bridge Street and waited for the light to change.

"Very good. The *Native Americans* lived in the forest along the banks of the Sankanac for thousands of years. At first, Coates was so scared of the Indians that he slept with a loaded flintlock musket at his side, but soon after, he realized that the natives were friendly. In just one winter he trapped 24 beavers."

"Wow, there aren't any beaver around here anymore. No wonder."

"Coates liked the place so much that he talked his friend James Starr into buying the land on this side of the creek. They called it the Mill Tract. We are actually walking its east border now. It started down there at the low bridge, then ran up Main Street past us to Church Street, at the top of the hill. Then it went right, past the post office, all the way to the Fountain Inn."

"You mean Pat's Pizza," the boy corrected him. The light changed and they crossed the street.

"Yes, to Pat's Pizza," the man repeated, smiling. When they got to the other side he continued, "From there, the line went north back to the creek, then back to the low bridge again. Can you picture that?"

"I think so. He would have owned all of Bridge Street." The boy pointed to the mural on their left. "The mural here, the movie theater, Borough Hall, all of it."

"Yes, except none of that was here back then. It was just quiet woods before Starr and his two sons started cutting down trees and gathering stone to build their home." The old man stopped in front of a well-kept two-story fieldstone farmhouse that seemed out of place next to the modern buildings with their dumpsters and fire escapes. It was like time had stopped here. In front was a small yard filled with green grass. "In fact," he said with pride, "this is the first house they built, way back in 1732."

"It is the original Starr farmhouse, the oldest house in Phoenixville. They also built a gristmill on the creek. It would have stood some-where over there." The boy followed his grandfather's hand as he pointed. "Just past where the foundry parking lot is now." Then they started walking in that direction.

The Original Starr Farmhouse
Built in 1732, this is the oldest structure in Phoenixville.

"Pop-pop, what's a grist mill?"

"Grist was the colonists' word for grain. You would take your corn or wheat and have it ground into flour for cooking. How do you think they managed to do that?"

"They ground it up between two big rocks called mill stones. You showed me one outside the Kimberton post office, remember? We fed the ducks, and you told me about how the water from the ponds went down a little chute to turn a water wheel."

"You have a good memory. I'm very impressed." The old man mussed the boy's hair. "Well, Starr built a dam upstream to make his own pond so that he would have a consistent source of water to power the mill. For a time, Starr and his two sons ran the mill, but business must not have been too good because soon they rented it to a man named Rowland Richards. Richards decided that business would pick up if more people knew where his mill was. So, he cut a path through the woods and all along the path carved the letters R.R.M. into the trees to show people the way to Rowland Richard's Mill."

The boy finished his ice cream and wiped his hands on his khaki shorts. "So, he put up the first billboards!"

The old man chuckled, "Yes, I suppose he did. Anyhow, over time Rowland started drinking, and his poor wife had to start doing more and more of the milling for him. They had a large family, and although she did the very best she could, she couldn't keep up with the bills. The county sheriff was called out to evict them from the mill. They gathered their meager worldly possessions and left. Having been abandoned by Rowland and not knowing where they would go or what they would do, Mrs. Richards stopped on the roadside, not far from where we are right now, her crying children gathered around her. She was so distraught that she turned back towards the mill and called upon God to put a hex upon it."

"A hex?"

"A curse. She made it so that no one who owned the mill would ever prosper. And, it seems to have worked. The Starr family sold the mill in 1748, and in just a few years, the sheriff would twice have to evict owners who could not meet their obligations. When the British army came through here in 1777, they took everything that wasn't nailed down. The mill kept changing hands until it was eventually sold to Benjamin Longstreth in 1786. You might say that Longstreth is the true father of Phoenixville."

"Really? Is that because he named it Phoenixville?"

"No, that wouldn't happen for another 50 years. Benjamin Longstreth bought up most of the land on the south side of the creek where Phoenixville now stands, one hundred and sixty-one acres in total. He built a sawmill just upstream from the gristmill. It probably would have been right over there, somewhere." He pointed towards the creek. "And he built a new, bigger dam to power it all. But, the reason I said he is the true father of Phoenixville is that, in 1790, he built a rolling and slitting mill. It was right there, where the foundry building is now." The boy turned his head in the direction his Grandfather pointed.

"What's a rolling and slitting mill?" the boy asked his Grandfather.

"Forges, like the one in Valley Forge, made iron bars from local ore. At the mill here, they would heat up the bars and then use big metal rollers to press the bars into thin sheets. The metal sheets were slit into long thin rods that were cut into short pieces and hand forged into nails. Longstreth called it the French Creek Nail Works."

"But what about the curse?"

"Funny you should ask. It wasn't long before there was a tremendous storm and the dam failed, resulting in a devastating flood. Mr. Longstreth fixed the dam and the damage to the nail works, but before long the dam broke again. This time, it washed the rolling and slitting mill completely away. All that was left after the water receded was a deep hole with several tons of iron at the bottom."

"How did they get the iron out of the hole?"

"They couldn't, so they just took the loss, filled in the hole, and started all over again. Longstreth was almost done rebuilding when the dam broke a third time and washed it all away again. Can you guess what he did then?"

"He got smart and gave up?"

The old man laughed. "I suppose he should have. Instead, he was determined to rebuild once more, only bigger and better than ever. He succeeded, but it cost him everything he had. In 1800, the land was put up at Sheriff's sale, yet again. And this time, it was sold to a man named Andrew Douglas. The curse caught up to the Douglas family soon after, as well. Mrs. Douglas fell from a wall, broke her neck, and died, and Mr. Douglas was forced to live out his remaining days in the Chester County almshouse."

"What's an almshouse?" the boy asked.

"The poorhouse. It was a place for people to go when they were broke," his grandfather explained, "which Douglas must have been because in 1802 the sheriff sold all Douglas's property to James McClintock, who ran the mills for the next seven years... when everything changed." The old man turned and started walking towards the foundry building.

The boy ran behind him shouting, "Changed? Changed how? Pop-pop, where are you going?!"

The old man walked a short distance and eased himself down onto the first available bench. His grandson caught up, picked up the library books his grandfather just set down, and took a seat next to him on the bench. He waited patiently, as his grandfather took a few deep breaths and cleared his throat before continuing.

"Up until then, each nail had to be cut and hammered by hand, which was very labor-intensive. But, a man named Thomas Odiorne invented a new kind of machine for making nails. He bought the French Creek Nail Works, installed his new machine, and began flooding the market with inexpensive, mass-produced nails."

"In 1813, a German engineer named Lewis Wernwag was hired as a superintendent to manage the nail works. Wernwag was known for designing and overseeing the construction of the largest single-span bridge ever constructed anywhere in the world at the time, and it was all made of wood. It went over the Schuylkill into Philadelphia."

"Anyway, Wernwag loved to build in stone even more than wood.

So, he replaced the wooden nail factory with a stone building. Then he constructed a stone aqueduct supported by sturdy arches to carry water from the dam. He also built a stone blacksmith shop and stone cooper shop, as well as many other stone buildings. He even built a house for himself with stone walls twice as thick as normal and solid walnut woodwork inside. Why, even the floors were wooden. Wernwag terraced the bank down to the creek with thick stone walls, as well, and even built an octagonal schoolhouse out of stone for the children of the workers."

The boy interrupted, "Two questions, Grandpa. What's a cooper, and where did he get all that stone from?"

"A cooper makes the barrels that are needed to hold all the nails. They got the stone from the steep bluff on the north side of the creek over there, behind that apartment building." The boy seemed satisfied with his answers, so the old man continued. "Lewis Wernwag is the one who renamed this place the Phoenix Iron Works."

"I know that story," the boy interjected excitedly. "He saw the sparks shooting out of the furnaces at night, and it reminded him of the mythical bird that dies and then rises from its own ashes. A firebird."

"Correct, and it was Wernwag who first proposed changing the name from Manavon to Phoenixville. The problem was, although a talented engineer, Wernwag wasn't a very good businessman. Eventually, he and all the other investors in the Phoenix Iron Works were compelled to sell their interests until just one man, George Thompson, owned it all. Wernwag was evicted from his castle on the hill, and Thompson moved in."

"When Thompson took over, the rolling mill had only one pair of rollers and one pair of rotary slitters, and everything was powered by a single water wheel. The entire output of the mill was maybe three tons a day. The iron was carried from the rolling mill to the nail factory on the back of just one donkey. There was only one furnace, and everything was heated by charcoal or bituminous coal. Do you know what that is?"

"No. What's bitnuminus coal?"

"*Bituminous* coal is soft coal. It doesn't burn as hot as hard anthracite coal. Anyway, the coal was set on fire, and when it was hot enough, the iron was placed on top until it was the perfect temperature, which was tricky because you could burn the iron and ruin it."

"You can burn iron? That sounds crazy."

"You can indeed, just like cookies in the oven. Anyway, Thompson enlarged the rolling mill, and he installed a steam engine to run the machinery when there was not enough water from the creek. He also erected a puddling furnace to convert pig iron to bar iron."

"Did the iron bars keep the pigs from playing in the puddles?"

"Ha, ha, ha... funny man. Pig iron is what you get when you smelt iron ore. It's iron, but it's so brittle that it would crack if you tried to work it. Puddling turns pig iron into malleable bar iron by cooking the carbon out of it. And, if you don't know, now you know." The old man smiled contentedly as he sat back.

"Ha, ha, ha... funny man," the boy responded with a roll of his eyes as he swung his feet back and forth from his perch on the bench seat. If he pointed his toes down, his sneakers barely touched the ground.

The old man looked around, taking in the beautiful day as he went on, "Thompson then went about buying up everything he could get his hands on. He bought the Starr farm at 148 acres, the Rhoades farm at 133 acres, and Phoenix Hill at 83 acres, as well as many smaller lots. Then, he started building houses so people could move here. They were all the same: one story high, with two rooms and no cellar. They built sixteen of those houses all around here and sold them for seventy-five dollars each. Housing was scarce, and people were poor. So, it wasn't uncommon for one house to have a dozen people living in it."

"Are any of them still standing?" the boy asked. "Maybe we could go see one."

"Sorry, champ. The last one of those houses was located about where the Diving Cat Studio is now, but it was torn down in the name of progress. The Thompsons built a company store up that way, as well, where the old Woolworths was, across from Steel City." The old man motioned back the way they had come towards the intersection of Main and Bridge. The boy nodded that he understood.

His grandfather continued, "This whole place was like its own little town, with its own money. The eighty men and women who worked here were paid with company checks, little colored cards that were worth anywhere from three cents up to five dollars. These cards were accepted at all the local establishments and taverns, such as the Fountain Inn and the General Pike. And, of course, they were accepted at the corner stores that were also owned by the Thompsons."

"You told me about the Corner Stores, but you never told me the Thompsons owned them."

"That's because you didn't know who the Thompsons were when I told you about the Corner Stores. But, yes, the Thompsons owned most of the town, small as it was."

They watched a family of five as they pedaled by on the bike path. The boy looked at his grandfather. "So, the curse was finally gone, then?"

"Not quite. In 1822, the dam gave way again, and once more they rebuilt it. This time, they dug all the way down to the bedrock, ten feet below the creek, and built it so strong that they thought it would last forever. About that time, the Thompsons shut down the gristmill and diverted all of the available waterpower to the iron works. Since they would no longer use the old mill, they sold it to pay their bills. What they did not expect was that the new owners would turn around and sell it to their biggest competitors, the Cumberland Works of Bridgeton, New Jersey, owned by Leaming, Whitaker, and Reeves."

"Reeves... like the park? I think I can see where this is going." The boy shrugged his shoulders, "So much for, 'keep your friends close and your enemies closer.'"

The old man's forehead creased, then his eyebrows raised. He cocked his head as he looked over at the boy seated on the bench next to him. "That was pretty quick."

The boy nodded, then looked around and said nonchalantly, "I have my moments."

"So you do. Well, the company sent Joseph Whitaker to Phoenixville to start operations at the Old Mill. He moved into the Starr farmhouse that we looked at earlier. Of course, the locals all knew about the curse and were just waiting for him to fail. But Joseph Whitaker wasn't about to let that happen. He ran a very tight ship. He was good with money and expected a lot from his employees." A tiger swallowtail flitted among the flowers next to the bench. The boy reached his finger out to touch it, but it fluttered away.

"By 1830, despite the fact that the Phoenix Iron Works was one of the largest nail factories in the nation, the town was just a small village cut out of pristine wilderness. The hills on the north side of the creek were still covered with dense forest and were full of animals. There weren't any bridges, just Jacob's Ford across the Schuylkill and another small ford across the French Creek, where the low bridge is today. So, to encourage growth in the neighborhood, boundaries were surveyed, land was sold, roads were laid out, houses were built, and the town slowly began to take shape."

"Sounds like they finally beat the curse."

"Don't you believe it. The winter of 1838 was very cold. For three months the snow kept piling up. The creeks were all iced up, and very little water was running. Then, on January 26th, 1839, a warm rain began and did not let up for a day and a half. The French Creek swelled to overflowing and threatened to sweep over the dam."

"Elias Day lived above the mill with his wife and children. Henry O'Brien and his sister, Susan, were also staying with them. When it looked like the dam might break, the women took the kids to high ground, but the men refused to leave. Mrs. Day returned to the mill to persuade them to leave, and while she was there the headgates of the canal exploded with a crash, and a torrent of water full of ice, logs, and debris surrounded the mill."

"That must have been so scary!" the boy exclaimed.

"You got that right," the old man agreed. "Susan crawled out of their second-story window onto the porch roof and yelled to some townsfolk for help. They threw her a rope from the bank, and she tied it around her waist. Good thing, too, because just then the mill started collapsing." The boy's eyes grew big as he listened intently, picturing the story playing out in his mind.

His grandfather continued, "The townspeople managed to pull Mrs. Day to the shore, but she was battered and unconscious. Henry O'Brien was strong from working at the mill. He fought the current and almost made it to the shore before a log hit him and swept him away. To keep from drowning, Elias Day grabbed hold of an ice floe and rode it down the creek all the way out into the Schuylkill. There, he was finally able to grab ahold of a tree sticking up from one of the little islands in the river. He was washed out around eleven in the morning, and they heard his cries for help until well after dark. The floodwater was so bad that there was no way anyone could get to him. When the waters finally receded, not a stone of the Old Mill remained. The powerful flood carved out a hole 14 feet deep in its place."

"Was *that* the end of the curse?" the boy asked hopefully.

"You'll have to be the judge of that. In 1838, the Philadelphia and Reading Railroad finished the Black Rock Tunnel, and soon trains from Pottsville were providing an abundant supply of anthracite coal to the Iron Works. This new supply of coal allowed them to build a blast furnace so that they could make their own iron by smelting locally obtained ore. The blast furnace turned out 30 tons of pig iron a week. To process it all, they built six new puddling furnaces and a new rolling mill powered by an eighty-horsepower steam engine."

"Then, in 1848 the nail factory burned to the ground along with all the machinery and 1,400 kegs of nails. The workers tried to put out the fire, but there was nothing they could do to stop it. A big old bell that hung in the factory to call the men to work tolled one last time as the factory came crashing down in the flames. The factory was not rebuilt. After 40 years as one of the nation's leading producers of nails, Phoenixville was about to change tracks, literally."

"The railroad's demand for iron rails was soaring. Phoenix Iron Works rolled out their first rails in 1846, and they were an instant success. Now, with the nail factory gone, they decided to focus their efforts on producing iron for the railroad full time. They built a new, even larger rolling mill and increased their workforce to 300 men. To house the new workers and their families, they built Nailer's Row."

"Hey, now I know why it's called that!" the boy exclaimed. "It's right over there!" He pointed to the rows of houses behind the foundry. "My friend Angelo lives in the house all the way on the other end, just before the high bridge."

The old man pushed himself to his feet. "When the Civil War started in 1861, the Union needed the best cannons they could get, so they ordered 1,400 Griffin Guns, a new type of cannon that was more accurate and safer to fire. The Griffin Gun is credited with helping the Union win the war."

He walked over to a series of beams set vertically into the concrete in a large sweeping arc. "Cannons may have saved the Union, but I believe that these columns are of far greater historical significance. Behold, the phenomenally fabulous Phoenix Column! Samuel Reeves invented it in 1862. Go ahead, take a close look and tell me what you see."

The boy went over to the towering iron beam and ran his fingers over it. "It's not square, like I expected. It's round and made up of different pieces." He walked a few feet to the next column, standing tall like a metal tree trunk growing out of the brick and concrete, and examined it. "This one is a little bigger and made up of more long sections, all bolted together."

"They're riveted," the old man said, "and because the columns were hollow, they were lighter and less expensive to manufacture and ship, while their circular shape made them incredibly strong. Reeves' columns are what allowed people around the world to build tall skyscrapers and long bridges."

"Is that why the park is named after him and why there is a statue of him there?"

"That's a big part of the reason, yes. These columns were all made in the foundry here. See that double-tiered roof? Those extra windows let light inside while allowing the intense heat from the furnaces to escape. Everything in that building was made from local materials. The walls are two feet thick and made of sandstone quarried from the cliffs on the other side of the river. The bricks were all made at the McAvoy brickyard, and the truss work that holds up the slate roof was fabricated on site, smelted, refined, and rolled right here in the mills. A few years later, they manufactured their first steel in this very building. There is a museum inside. Would you like to check it out?"

"Okay, I'll race you to the door!" The boy started running towards the front of the building. The old man let him run. His racing days were over, but he still remembered how good it felt to be that young. Now, he found his pleasure in watching the boy's seemingly boundless energy and inquisitiveness. The boy disappeared around the corner of the building, but the old man did not hurry. He walked slowly, enjoying the fresh air and warm sun on his thin, wrinkled skin. When he finally got to the entrance, he found his grandson waiting proudly, with a shining smile on his face, holding the door open for him.

"Thank you," the old man said, tipping an imaginary hat as he went in. "You are a gentleman and a scholar." Inside, part of the building was sectioned off for the Schuylkill River Heritage Center Museum. Inlaid on the floor was a map of the Schuylkill River, from its beginnings in Tamaqua to its mouth where it empties into the Delaware River. "Can you find Phoenixville?" the old man asked.

The boy looked at the map, then pointed at a red area next to a sharp bend in the river. The old man smiled. "That's right."

The boy scanned the room. "Hey, look! There's another map painted on the wall over here, and it's interactive." The boy went over and pushed the buttons. Each one told about a different part of the river by presenting information and pictures on a screen. After a few minutes, they moved on. "Here's another Phoenix column."

"These columns played a major role in the industrial revolution and were shipped all around the world," his grandfather stated. "Look over here. This picture shows how columns were used in the Washington Monument. And here is a picture of the tower Samuel Reeves designed and planned to use to demonstrate the strength of his columns. It would have been more than twice as high as the pyramids. Unfortunately, Reeves never built it because it was too expensive. However, ten years after Gustav Eiffel saw this poster, he built his Eiffel Tower."

The boy went up to a glass case that held memorabilia from the Iron Company. Inside, a brass bell rested on a cylindrical wooden stand. The boy read the label. "It says this was the school bell that hung in the octagon schoolhouse until it was demolished in 1949."

"That was right next to the company office. The Reeves family knew the value of education and thought that all the kids in the neighborhood should go to school. Do you see those wooden sandals there? Workers wore them over their leather boots to protect their feet from getting burned on the hot floors."

"Hey, Pop-Pop, what is the difference between iron and steel?"

"Hay is for horses, young man." The boy rolled his eyes at the pun, so his grandfather went on, "Iron is a metal, which means it forms naturally. In fact, it's the most abundant element on Earth. But, you won't find steel naturally occurring anywhere on Earth because steel is an alloy. That means it is a mixture of metals that is man-made."

"How do you know so much about the steel company, Pop-Pop?"

"Our family worked in this mill for three generations. When your great-great-grandfather came here from Hungary, he got a job as a day laborer. He couldn't even speak English, but the mill was an equal opportunity employer. It didn't matter what color you were or where you were from, you could get a job at the mill. The 1900 census listed him as a boarder living on Cinder Street."

"Cinder Street? Where is that? I never heard of it."

"It was renamed Walnut Street. Anyway, 40 years later, I grew up just a block away, on Morgan Street. I started working here at the mill in 1960 when I turned 18 and worked here until they closed down over 25 years later. Over 2,000 employees worked around the clock, 24/7. This place never slept."

"2,000 people worked in this building? It's not *that* big!"

"The foundry building was important, but it was only a small part of the steel company. Here, look at this map. There were buildings all over. There was a machine shop just on the other side of Main Street that was easily twice as big as this building. There were train tracks that ran right inside. Then, there was the girder shop on the other side of the Gay Street Bridge. It was so enormous that ten foundry buildings could have fit inside."

"Wow. What happened, Pop-pop? Was it the curse?"

"I think that curse, if there ever was one, washed away a long time ago along with the old mill. After World War II, there were many more steel mills than there were before the war, so Phoenix Steel faced a lot of competition. People also started using more aluminum and reinforced concrete in their buildings. When Phoenix Steel officially closed down in 1987, I was one of the last employees left. We fenced off the property and demolished most of the buildings. This building was left standing, but it was abandoned and vandalized for over a decade. It made me very happy when it was renovated as part of the Schuylkill River Heritage Project."

"I'm glad they saved it, too. I think history is pretty cool. I like knowing about the places around here."

"So do I, champ. Before we head back, they have a short video about the history of the Iron and Steel Company with narration from people who actually worked there. Would you like to see it?"

"Are you in it?" the boy asked hopefully.

The old man looked down at his grandson and smiled. "I suppose we'll just have to watch it and see."

Epilogue

After Phoenix Steel closed in 1987, other smaller manufacturing firms soon followed. Like many old steel towns in Pennsylvania, Phoenixville experienced some difficult economic times. However, like the mythical bird that gives the town its name, Phoenixville has since risen from the ashes. Philadelphia's suburban expansion has helped to revitalize the town, and now Phoenixville is growing and prospering once again.

Today, the town of Phoenixville relies less on the manufacturing of nails and rails and more on its artsy vibe to attract both visitors craving relaxation and new residents looking to put down roots. Bridge Street, the town's main drag, offers an almost urban atmosphere with its quaint mix of wine-tasting rooms, restaurants, distilleries, craft breweries, and distinctive shops and boutiques.

The original Phoenix Iron Works foundry has been converted into an interpretive center and catering facility. This repurposed building serves as a symbol of how this gritty community reinvented itself to become a popular place to live, work, and play for a new generation of residents.

~ Final Thoughts ~

The location we call Phoenixville has quite a history. Enjoy your time here because it has an equally incredible history ahead of it. Someday, you and the house you know so well will be gone. Perhaps a new structure will be built in its place, maybe a residence or a business. However, someday even that structure and whoever builds it will be gone as well, and the landscape will change yet again. The creations of man will crumble and be reclaimed. It is inevitable and natural that someday, far in the future, new and strange animals and perhaps even new and different kinds of people will dwell in the place that we once called home. Will they know of us? Will there be any record of our existence? Would they even care? Maybe. By then, though, we will have become just another tale in the long history of the special little place on planet Earth that we affectionately call *Phoenixville*.

~ Photo and Illustration Credits ~

Cover Design: *Main Street, Phoenixville PA,* postcard, 1905.
From the collection of John Keenan. Restored by Joe Varady.

All illustrations/photos by Joe Varady unless listed otherwise.

In the US, any work published before January 1, 1925 is in the
public domain.

Pg 76: Paine, Thomas. *Common Sense.* 1776. Web. 11 March 2021.

Pg. 111: *Canal boat built to transport anthracite on the Schuylkill
Canal.* Circa 1890. Web. 11 March 2021.

Pg. 112: *Original logo for the Reading Railroad.* Web. 11 March 2021.

Pg. 114: *Beadle's Half Dime Library, Vol 8.* 1881. Web. 11 March 2021.

Pg 117: Swartz. *The Wild Bunch.* Texas. 1900. Web. 11 March 2021.

Pg. 123: *The Phoenix Hotel.* Circa 1900. Web. 11 March 2021.

Pg. 124: *F.W. Woolworth Co., Phoenixville, PA.* Postcard.
From the collection of John Keenan.

Pg. 127: *Colonial Theater, Phoenixville, PA.* Postcard.
From the collection of John Keenan.

Pg. 129: *Trolley in Phoenixville.* Circa 1917. Web. 11 March 2021.

Pg. 134: United Press International, *Handcuff King Releases Himself
from Straight Jacket.* Postcard. 1919. Web. 11 March 2021.

Pg. 137: *Houdini Performs the East India Needle Trick.* 1924.
Web. 11 March 2021.

Pg. 139: *Houdini in a Safe.* 1924. Web. 11 March 2021.
Composite by Joe Varady.

Pg. 162: *Colonial Run-Out.* Composite of photos taken by Barry
Taglieber and Joe Varady. 2021.

~ *Bibliography* ~

Introduction - Our Geologic Past

Hoskins, Donald M., et al. *Fossil Collecting in Pennsylvania.* Pennsylvania, Bureau of Topographic and Geologic Survey, 1983.

Chapter One - New Arrivals: The Tale of the Ice Age Hunters

Fagan, Brian M. *Ancient North America: the Archaeology of a Continent.* Langara College, 2019.

Sevon, William D., et al. *Pennsylvania and the Ice Age.* Pennsylvania Geological Survey, 2005.

"PHMC Pre-1681: The Eve of Colonization." *Pre-1681: The Eve of Colonization | PHMC > Pennsylvania History,* www.phmc.state.pa.us/portal/communities/pa-history/pre-1681.html.

Chapter Two - The First European: The Tale of Charles Pickering

Annals of Phoenixville and Its Vicinity: from the Settlement to the Year 1871, Giving the Origin and Growth of the Borough, with Information Concerning the Adjacent Townships of Chester and Montgomery Counties and the Valley of the Schuylkill, by Samuel W. Pennypacker, Esq. Published by Bavis & Pennypacker, 1872.

Lewis, Joseph J. *History of Chester County.* 1894.

J. Smith Futhey and Gilbert Cope, *History of Chester County,* J.B. Lippincott & Co., Philadelphia, 1881.

Lewis, John Frederick, *The History of an Old Philadelphia Land Title,* Philadelphia, 1934.

"Philadelphia History: Dock Street." *Ushistory.org,* Independence Hall Association, www.ushistory.org/Philadelphia/street_dock.htm.

"Philadelphia." *Wikipedia*, Wikimedia Foundation, 15 Mar. 2021, en.wikipedia.org/wiki/Philadelphia#History.

Chapter Three - A Clash of Cultures: The Tragic Tale of Indian Rock

Annals of Phoenixville and Its Vicinity: from the Settlement to the Year 1871, Giving the Origin and Growth of the Borough, with Information Concerning the Adjacent Townships of Chester and Montgomery Counties and the Valley of the Schuylkill, by Samuel W. Pennypacker, Esq. Published by Bavis & Pennypacker, 1872.

Eshleman, H. Frank. *Lancaster County Indians: Annals of the Susquehannocks and Other Indian Tribes of the Susquehanna Territory from about the Year 1500 to 1763, the Date of Their Extinction. An Exhaustive and Interesting Series of Historical Papers Descriptive of Lancaster County's Indians Prior to and during the Advent of the Paleface.* Forgotten Books, 2015.

Chapter Four - Till the Cows Come Home: Lizzie Buckwalter

Annals of Phoenixville and Its Vicinity: from the Settlement to the Year 1871, Giving the Origin and Growth of the Borough, with Information Concerning the Adjacent Townships of Chester and Montgomery Counties and the Valley of the Schuylkill, by Samuel W. Pennypacker, Esq. Published by Bavis & Pennypacker, 1872.

Charlestown Historical Society Webpage, *Charlestown.org*, www.charlestown.org/ct-org/cthst/ctin_the_beginning.asp.

Chapter Five - The Redcoats are Coming! Jonathan Coates

Annals of Phoenixville and Its Vicinity: from the Settlement to the Year 1871, Giving the Origin and Growth of the Borough, with Information Concerning the Adjacent Townships of Chester and Montgomery Counties and the Valley of the Schuylkill, by Samuel W. Pennypacker, Esq. Published by Bavis & Pennypacker, 1872.

Chapter Six - Freedom Road: The Tale of Deacon Armour

Kashatus, William C. *Just over the Line: Chester County and the Underground Railroad.* Chester County Historical Society, 2002.

Jirik, Mike. "The Role of Violence in the Abolitionist Movement." *AAIHS*, 19 Aug. 2020, www.aaihs.org/the-role-of-violence-in-the-abolitionist-movement.

Jackson, Kellie Carter. *Force and Freedom: Black Abolitionists and the Politics of Violence.* University of Pennsylvania, 2020.

Chapter Seven - Birth of a Legend: The Tale of the Sundance Kid

"New Addition to the Sundance Kid Mystery." *Phoenixville Chamber of Commerce*, 23 June 2017, phoenixvillechamber.org/news-events/news/new-addition-sundance-kid-mystery/.

Chapter Eight - Escape at the Colonial: The Great Houdini

Cox, John. *Houdini in 1916*, 1 Jan. 1970, www.wildabouthoudini.com/2016/01/houdini-in-1916.html.

Brunner, William C. "The Spring City Trolley." *Limerick-Royersford-Spring City, PA Patch*, Patch, 9 Sept. 2011, patch.com/pennsylvania/limerick/bp--the-spring-city-trolley-2.

Chapter Nine - Hollywood on the Pickering: The Tale of the Blob

McKendry, Rebekah. "The Supposedly True Story Behind the Classic Film THE BLOB!" *The 13th Floor,* 27 Feb. 2018, www.the13thfloor.tv/2015/10/21/the-movie-the-blob-is-based-on-a-supposedly-true-event-read-the-real-story-behind-this-classic-film/.

Inglis-Arkell, Esther. "The Blob was Based on a True Story." *io9*, io9, 16 Dec. 2015, io9.gizmodo.com/the-true-story-behind-the-blob-1623120977.

"Blob Town (2010)." *YouTube*, YouTube, 7 Nov. 2016, www.youtube.com/watch?v=RNCzzHBnPqg.

Lambie, Ryan, et al. "The Strange History of The Blob Movies." *Den of Geek*, 29 Jan. 2015, www.denofgeek.com/movies/the-strange-history-of-the-blob-movies/.

"The Blob." *IMDb*, IMDb.com, www.imdb.com/title/tt0051418/trivia.

Chapter Ten - The Curse of the Old Mill: Phoenix Steel

Annals of Phoenixville and Its Vicinity: from the Settlement to the Year 1871, Giving the Origin and Growth of the Borough, with Information Concerning the Adjacent Townships of Chester and Montgomery Counties and the Valley of the Schuylkill, by Samuel W. Pennypacker, Esq. Published by Bavis & Pennypacker, 1872.

"Schuylkill River Heritage Center Part 2 Virtual Tour - Phoenix Iron and Steel Company." *YouTube*, YouTube, 29 Sept. 2020, www.youtube.com/watch?v=8d_9_HnOuus.

The author, Joe Varady Jr., and his father, Joe Varady Sr. (2009).

~ About the Author ~

Born in the Phoenixville Hospital in 1969, Joe Varady is the fourth generation of the Varady family to live in this town. Growing up, his father often taught him interesting stories about Phoenixville and its surrounding areas.

Joe graduated from Gettysburg College in 1991 with a degree in studio art before attending West Chester University, where he earned a master's degree in elementary education. After graduate school, he used his art skills to enhance his effectiveness as a 5th grade teacher at Barkley Elementary School from 1994-2004, when he quit to become a full-time dad to his two kids, Cosmos and Kayla.

Joe enjoys sharing his knowledge of local history. *Tales of Phoenixville*, his first foray into historical fiction, fulfills his desire to continue sharing Phoenixville's rich and exciting history with members of the community. He hopes that this book will serve to educate and entertain both current as well as future generations.

Joe lives in Phoenixville with his wife, Kathy, and two children. Joe holds a sixth-degree black belt and is the founder and chief instructor of Satori Dojo Martial Arts, which he founded in 1994. A national champion weapons fighter, he is also the author of several books on the martial arts including *The Art and Science of Staff Fighting* (2016) and *The Art and Science of Stick Fighting* (2020).

Cover: Looking north on Main Street, 1905.